STAND YOUR GROUND

Raeder Lomax

This novel is a work of fiction. The characters, incidents, and dialogue are drawn from the author's imagination and are not to be construed as real. The author holds all rights to this work. It is illegal to reproduce this novel without written expressed consent from the author, except in the case of brief quotations embodied in critical articles or reviews.

Copyright © 2015 Raeder Lomax
All rights reserved.
Cover Design: Evan Morris Cohen
Cover Photo: ©Godlis

ISBN: 1514888416
ISBN 13: 9781514888414
Library of Congress Control Number: 2015917470
CreateSpace Independent Publishing Platform
North Charleston, South Carolina

"Stand your ground" simply means that, if you reasonably believe that you face imminent death, serious bodily injury, rape, kidnapping, or (in most states) robbery, you can use deadly force against the assailant, even if you have a perfectly safe avenue of retreat.
—*Washington Post*, Eugene Volokh, June 27, 2014

CHAPTER ONE

When Lawton Gibbs walked out of prison after serving the bottom half of a twenty-year bid in Florida's Union Correctional Facility at Starke, the only thing he had before him was a lot of wide- open space, and even that wasn't enough. The caged voices that had day in and day out bounced off the prison walls were still ringing in his ears. He was told at release: "Give it a few days. It will be like you were never here." Then he was handed an "Ex-Offender" ID card and sent on his way.

Lawton walked the two miles to SR-16 and waited until a black F-150 Raptor with yellow flames on the quarter panels came riding out of the piercing midday summer sun. Its Widow All-Terrain tires scattered dirt off the road and pulled to a dead stop. A seventeen-year-old girl with light brown skin and a body that was frightening to a man just out of lockup said, "Are you Lawton Gibbs?"

Lawton cautiously stared at Crystal, whom he hadn't seen in ten years. "I am," not forgetting that she had once called him "Uncle Lawton" and wanting to tell Roy LaHood, her father, (still in Starke and to be released in a few days), how strange freedom felt and how much his little girl had grown up.

Crystal, sounding more like a prison guard, said, "Get in," as she unlocked the passenger door, thinking he too looked different. He was grayer, the resin of age now upon him with eyes as faded as an echo, but Father Time hadn't washed away the cool easy stare that could make other people less easy.

Crystal said, "What are you waiting for?"

Lawton didn't need permission to enter, but ten years of being told what to do was still with him.

He got into the truck. Found the seat adjuster. Shut the door. Still wary that a uniform would come and tell him to return to his cell. Crystal put the truck in gear and drove off. Neither knew exactly what to say. Crystal felt like she was on a blind date with someone the wrong age. Lawton felt like a mutt rescued from the pound on its way to a new home.

She said, "No bag?"

"Just what I wore in." He almost smiled, but lost grip of his humor as he stared at the girl in the pink stretch tank top. She had more than enough cleavage, but it was her mother's deceptively sleepy green eyes that only a kiss could close that reminded him of what he had been missing all those years stuck behind bars.

They headed onto I-95 south.

Crystal said, "My mother wants to talk to you about something."

"And just what would that be?"

"Well, something's bugging her and you know how she gets." Forgetting Lawton hadn't seen Roberta in ten years. "And she only wants to do it in person, not on the phone."

Lawton said, "I'm going to Palm Beach, first. I'll talk to your mother when I get settled in." He reached for the generic-brand cigarettes on the dashboard. "May I?"

"Go ahead."

Lawton lit up. He was thinking about Mrs. Leyland Johnson and her late husband, whose genius had been in grasping the intricate and arcane world of law, which had enabled him to lead the charge on Wall Street to deregulate the banking industry in the late 1990s. His goal was to consolidate its lobbying powers and ease the psychological barrier of crony pilfering. Mrs. Johnson's contribution to the cause was putting Lawton behind bars.

For ten years, up and down the Eastern Seaboard, Lawton Gibbs and Roy LaHood had been known as the Four-Minute Gang, until a fateful night when a distressed Mrs. Johnson was about to swallow a handful of pills. A man dressed in black, from head to toe, appeared in her bedroom doorway. He was on his way to her dresser when he reached over: "I think we should talk."

She looked up from the rumpled sheets touching the floor. "Who are *you*?"

Lawton took the barbiturates from her hand. "Your savior."

Their lives changed forever after.

Crystal said, "Who's this woman?"

"Somebody."

"One who put you in jail?"

Lawton said, "You always drive this fast?"

"You wanna get to Palm Beach?"

"Alive, I do."

Keeping her foot to the pedal. "Well, you can forget about Audrey." Thinking of all the letters Lawton had written her while wasting away in prison. Not one of them opened. Wondering if he had any idea. "She won't have nothing to do with you, but then you already know that," almost making it a question.

Lawton said, "I hear she and Julia got a nice bungalow at Surfside Colony."

"Ya got big ears."

Lawton kept his eyes on I-95. Not yet used to being in something faster than a cell cot.

Crystal said, "Audrey's had several boyfriends in the past ten years."

Lawton pretended not to hear.

"Some real serious, too. This one dude all they did was to cuddle and walk on the beach. Ten years younger than Audrey, too. They'd make out for hours till the moon came out."

"You're gonna put your foot through the floorboard, you don't let up."

"He used to make Julia laugh until it hurt."

"How long have you been driving?"

"Not as long as you was in prison," enjoying Lawton's pain. Crystal passed another car. "Isn't Palm Beach where that old lady lives? One with all the money who put you into jail? Or do you have some other girlfriend who's ninety?"

"You're going over a hunnert."

Crystal let silence, the third passenger, weigh in as she pulled the truck into the middle lane. She passed a crawler then gunned it.

Lawton pressed his feet hard to the floorboard. He said, "I hear your mother's coming to visit your father."

"What about it?"

"It's the first time she been to Starke the five years he been there. Why all of a sudden?"

"That's their business."

"You're not the least curious as to why your mother's visiting him when he's getting out in just a few days?"

"She's an idiot."

"Not getting along with her?"

"Nobody gets along with my mother."

Lawton agreed. Roberta was like a snake you find under a garden chair with its mouth wide open and tail rattling. "I would say your father's lucky he's getting out of prison."

"Whaddya mean *lucky*?"

"I mean how that attorney of his, that Jenny Sullivan, how she got the courts to reverse his sentence because of that Stand Your Ground law not applied properly the first trial," grinning wide as a bear trap. "But then I didn't mind having an old friend keeping me company the last five years. I hear tell your mother's moved up to the front office of that gentleman's lounge—the Tote Him Pole Club?" Looking at Crystal to see if he got the name right.

"If you mean pole dancing, she finished with it long ago."

"I heard something happened between her and that Ronnie Harrison fella who owns it."

Crystal turned to Lawton long enough to let him know he was barking up the wrong tree.

He said, "What's this about your mother and that Ronnie Harrison splitting up?"

"All I know is that without my mother Ronnie Harrison is nothing. She runs the whole place. Keeps everything in order except for that creepy bartender, Marty Bannister, who's a drug dealer and a leech. Any woman within ten miles of him should be armed and warned."

Crystal cut to the right, passed a slowpoke, then eased back into the inside lane.

Lawton said, "You ever hear of signaling?"

"Keep your foot off the dashboard," wiping it. Letting him know she liked her truck spick-and-span.

"So it has to do with Ronnie Harrison—your mother coming up to Starke to visit your daddy. Something she wants and in a hurry."

"When you see her, y'all can talk all about it."

"I hear my wife's quite the star now at the club."

"You're sure about that?"

"Sure, I'm sure."

"Julia's the one who's the star. Not your *ex-wife*."

"*Julia's* the star?"

Crystal helped him out: "Your daughter. *Remember?*"

The last time he had seen Julia, she was ten years old, and that was how he still saw her. Trying to get the idea of Julia pole dancing out of his head was like trying to hold onto a tree in the middle of a hurricane. "What about her?"

"Don't let that ash fall."

Lawton tipped the cigarette out the window. "*What* about her?"

Crystal said, "When you see Julia, you can ask her. That's if they ever let you in the bungalow."

"What about Audrey?"

"Oh, she works the Executive Room."

"She's an executive?"

Crystal laughed. "Not exactly."

"What do you mean 'Not exactly'?"

"Takes care of customers."

"Customer relations?"

"That's a good way of putting it," Crystal said.

"Putting what?"

"Slow dancing."

"*Slow* dancing?"

"Hugs."

"The hell is hugs?"

"I just told ya."

"You didn't tell me nothing."

"That's because ya don't fucking listen."

"Watch your mouth, Crystal. I'm getting tired of it."

"*You* wanna go back to prison?"

"*You* wanna get smacked?"

Crystal pulled a Browning three-eighty from under her seat. She cut over to the center lane, passed the Buick Lacrosse with the snowbird asleep in the passenger seat, mouth wide open, and then back into the inside lane.

Lawton, his eye on the gun, "Look, I'm sorry. It was wrong of me to say that to you, but then you haven't been very pleasant."

"You're the one who hasn't been pleasant."

Lawton said, "You're father and I never once carried a weapon on a job. All a gun does is to escalate a situation."

"What am I supposed to do to a crazy person who wants to harm or rape me? *Let* him?"

"When was the last time that happened, Crystal?"

"It's the first time I'm worried about."

"You're gonna spend the rest of your life worrying about something that'll probably never happen."

"That's what *you* say."

Lawton sat back. He was in no mood to argue. There was no point. "You dance, too?"

"Yeah, I dance, but I'm into Bill T. Jones. Modern ballet. I'm a choreographer."

Eyeing her for a moment, "You don't look like a ballet dancer."

"Whaddya *mean* I don't look like a ballet dancer?"

Lawton looked down at her seat. "If I told you, you'd pull out that gun again."

CHAPTER TWO

Crystal turned into a roadside diner. Lawton felt odd standing outside the Raptor all on his own. No prison official telling him where to go. No gang member with a favor or *else*. He watched all the free people—still thinking of *them* as free—do something as simple as getting out of a car. Opening a menu. Free to make a choice. He glimpsed a cute waitress by the window adding up a bill, not worrying that her back wasn't covered. No one to mark or avoid. No open toilet. No one's blood to wipe.

Crystal and Lawton took the first window booth facing the highway. The waitress beelined over in her gummy shoes ready to get things going. She smiled, but the rest of her face showed little else. She handed them menus and said, "Hi there," as if the words were worn out and had holes in them. "The specials of the day are grilled—"

Crystal put up a hand. "Give us a minute."

"Coffee while ya think it over?"

Lawton nodded.

Crystal said, "Sweet tea for me."

The waitress left.

Lawton opened his menu. The lists of food overwhelmed him. There was an endless roll call of platters and sandwiches, open and closed, fried or grilled. The low-fat specials had the number of calories for all the snowbirds and tourists. There were so many things to choose Lawton had to start with what he didn't want, and there wasn't a lot of that after eating prison fare for ten years. Moments later the waitress rolled over with the coffee and sweet tea, ready for a second try.

Crystal said, "He just got out of prison, so this is sort of new to him."

Lawton found little humor in the remark.

The waitress tapped her order pad with the end of her pen, but Lawton was staring out the window, lost in thought. He was back in the prison yard the day when the light had gone out of his life.

Roy said, "You look paler than a ghost," as they walked along the perimeter.

Lawton said, "As far as Audrey and Julia are concerned, I'm dead." He showed Roy the other missive. "This is from that Mrs. Johnson."

Roy said, "I suppose that woman gonna give you half her fortune 'cause she sorry for putting you away all these years."

"Read the letter and tell me what you think."

Roy took the letter. "I already know what I think," as he examined the fancy hand-engraved bruised stationery. Mrs. Johnson's script was even and level. Words didn't drop off or get crammed at the end of the page. There were no cross outs, misspellings, or hesitations. No sense that Mrs. Johnson was thinking it out while she was writing. Roy noticed that the ink was water based: one of those classic fountain pens. It reminded him of the letters his granddad Beau used to write home during the Jazz Age when he was working on the train. Roy read those old letters many times over about all the different towns and folks Beau had met on-board with trunks that opened like cabinets. It was a world Roy knew only by way of his granddad's slow hard spelling, but it was a world as real to him as prison wire. Roy looked up from the letter, just for a breather, memory lane having taken him too far away. Then he read Mrs. Johnson's letter.

Dear Lawton,

    I'm sorry to have taken so long to answer you. Thank you for your kind words. They were, in their simplicity, a breath of fresh air. I've been under great pressure the past few years, and rather than follow my conscience, I did what other people wanted, but that is the past. I want to tell you that I haven't forgotten all your kindness, especially how you were able to express your thoughts so deeply to me the night I nearly took my life. You allowed me to say and feel what had been troubling me for years. I had truly come to believe that if there were people who cared for me, they had all vanished from my life. You've changed that. I now see those years, with my husband Leyland and his people, as a time of personal shame that go all the way back to when I was a young woman in Turkey. (You do remember how we spoke of that cruel and ignominious incident.) I've always lived in men's shadows, and they've gladly let me spoil myself into oblivion; nevertheless, I always felt that it was my right to share in Leyland's power, but I was never afforded equal status. My opinions on business and affairs of state were considered exiguous froth. After years of being denied access, I had lost all ambition, but I hadn't lost what I had learned from the men around me. I copiously kept notes in my journal of how they went about their affairs and executed their designs of pushing and nudging the government and its lawmakers to keep the legislative process clear for their investments. One day, in the future, I knew I, too, would need this knowledge, and when Leyland died, I became a force in business that no one had expected. Yet despite that, I struggled with the pros and cons concerning our friendship and, dare I say, beyond it. You and I are of different backgrounds, but it shouldn't ring falsely to say that each of us has had a hard life. Some may think that privilege isn't a burden; yet, I can rarely trust anyone who wants to befriend me. You were different. You came to me in my desperate state and took the drugs out of my hands, and soon we were talking about our fears, our utter sense of loneliness, and the world's inability to accept that our only true companion on earth is the ticktock of time and all that it drowns out. I admit that I had spoken more of this than you during those few but intensely passionate moments we had spent together. I soon rediscovered a part of myself that I had lost long ago: the self-worth that I had let slip away that night in Turkey when I was just twenty-one years old. You gave me back my self-respect, despite the fact that with all your kindness and consideration you stole nearly five million dollars of jewelry from me. So, at first I was guarded, unsure, feeble in my attempts to speak, more so to trust you despite the days we spent together when I loved you like nothing else in the world. I remember when I had asked you what it was that had made you happy, had set you free, you replied: "Self-worth." Something you couldn't buy; yet, something that was as easily accessible as a dream, if I would only allow myself to let it happen. Well, I have been dreaming, but awake, and now I have the courage to ask you to renew our friendship and rekindle the moment when you had unexpectedly come into my bedroom dressed in black from head to toe and changed my life. I am ready to move on, but I must warn you: should anyone have your ear and speak unkindly of me that I am a fool or an

easy target, make haste to disown those notions. I quickly detect deceit and deal with it just as effectively. I shall counter any thrust against my person or property with deadly force. But enough of that. I come with love. Do not let our difference of age tamper with reason. None of us is getting any younger. If you should still be disinclined to continue our relationship, after all these years, then let it be known that I have spoken honestly and freely from the heart and with a memory of a love so dearly missed that I shudder to even think of it and start suffering again.
Katherine Johnson (your Kathy)

Roy looked up from the letter. "I wanna see that picture of her." Roy took the photo out of Lawton's hand. Then he handed it back to him. "If she's a day under a hunnert, you're lucky."

"Roy, that woman's not even eighty."

"Maybe, but she like a peach been sitting on a window sill all summer long."

"Roy, I'm getting out of this prison in a few days."

"So am I."

"I can either get a job minimum wage and starve or—"

"What?"

Prisoners were leaving the yard.

"Take opportunity when it comes."

Roy stared at him the way a hiker does when he walks out of the woods and finds himself peering down the edge of a mile-long cliff. Roy said, "Take it, but beware. This woman is dangerous." They melded in with the rest of the inmates.

Lawton turned away from the diner booth window and said to the waitress, "I'll have coffee."

The waitress said, "Yeah, but what're you having to eat?"

"That's all I'm having," all he could afford.

CHAPTER THREE

They left the diner and drove on down to North Ocean Boulevard, Palm Beach, which was just a stone's throw from the ocean. Crystal, tired of riding up and down, said, "You're sure this is where that woman lives?"

"I know this area inside out. Your father and I spent days studying it before we went in. The Johnson house should be right there up the road."

Crystal drove on a bit. Lawton said, "Pull over."

"Why?"

"I got a feeling what we're looking for ain't no longer here."

"You just spoke to the old lady on the phone."

Lawton was already out of the truck. He found the access steps from the beach that he and Roy had used for the burglary, ten years earlier. Even the dead brush, where they had hidden their motorized raft, was just off to the side.

Crystal tossed a matchstick outside the truck window. "Maybe she's just messing with a man down on his luck."

Lawton said, "She's a hard woman, not a cruel woman."

A black Bentley Mulsanne rolled down the boulevard like it was aiming for a tenpin.

Lawton said, "I think I found her."

The big sedan pulled to a stop. The driver, dressed in livery, exited the car and walked his paces around the big loaf and opened the rear passenger door. He extended a gloved hand.

Lawton stepped on his cigarette and said to Crystal, "Wait here."

A tall, lean Southern woman stepped out of the Bentley. She was wearing a sleeveless summer dress with tiny interlocking patterns of red and gold angled lines with bursts of blue and silver. A thick gold necklace offset the tint of her dyed hair, once strawberry blond, but it was her Charleston pedigree that was as firm as the monuments in the Confederate harbor and as enduring as the memory of defeat that set her apart. Her yearning eyes, cloudier with time, still had as much proof as a bottle of Three Feathers on a reckless night. She stood by the edge of the Bentley and studied the man who had once robbed and then saved her. He seemed grayer, older, quieter in the eyes, more to her liking, as the ocean, breaking on shore, chipped away at the silence. Mrs. Johnson made the first move by stepping outside the perimeter of her car.

Lawton quietly said, "The house is gone, Kathy," as he turned toward the empty lot.

She said, "I had it torn down."

"Why?"

"When Leyland died, so did the house."

"Where do you live now?"

"Jupiter Beach."

"Why did you give me this address?"

"This is where we first met. I needed to see you here one more time." Thinking Lawton needed some new clothing, a bath, and a sharp razor. The chauffeur opened the rear passenger door of the Mulsanne. "You do understand that I couldn't be seen picking you up at that prison." Mrs. Johnson got in the car and waited. "Are you coming?"

CHAPTER FOUR

Roberta LaHood held the prison visitation dress code in one hand, her telephone to her ear in the other. She said to her husband, Roy, in lockup, "What about these rules?"

"What about them?"

"*Roy*, this here's a *long* list. You think I can remember it all?"

"You gotta abide by it if you want to visit a federal penitentiary."

"These are more than dress rules, Roy. Says: 'No hats, caps, scarves, headbands, sunglasses, wigs, jewelry, or medication unless it's life sustaining or for medical wear. Dresses and skirts must be knee length or longer. No button-up, wraparound, or sheer see-through fabric dresses or skirts.'" She stopped. "'Must wear a complete set of undergarments.' Do they check?"

"Roberta, you don't wear a complete set?"

"That's not what I mean."

"That's what *they* mean."

She looked at the other side of the form. "What's this about 'No green money'?"

"What about it?"

"There's some *other* color?"

"Roberta. This, a prison. They fussy which hand you pee with."

She went on, "'No tank tops, halter tops, low-cut blouses, sheer material, see-through pants. Capri pants must be calf length.' They mean Dolce & Gabbana or Emilio Pucci?"

"They mean everyone."

"Roy, I'm beginning to not like this whole idea."

"It was your idea to come up here."

"Yeah, but they're treating *me* like the criminal."

"Look, Roberta, my time is up. You decide to visit, you go through the gate. Then you sign something. They give you a pass. Box to put all your valuables. There's a metal detector. Invisible ink they put on your hand you push under a light. Then they move you on down to my level, where we sit in a booth and talk. Or you wait till I get out Wednesday. We'll have all the time in the world." Waiting for a response. "Roberta—? You still there?"

The next day, Roberta looked like she had crawled through a drainpipe. A double-cut window partition separated her from Roy. Everything else was shut, barred, bolted, or screened. A thick, penetrating sour smell made her cover her nose. She pulled up a chair, but a sticky film coated her fingers. She wiped it off then wrapped a tissue around the phone handle and cautiously put it by her ear without touching it. "How the hell ya live in a dump like this, Roy?"

"One day at a time."

"I'd lose my mind if I had to stay here one night."

"Many have."

Roberta turned to the guard then back to Roy. "I'm gonna make this short, because I don't think I can stay here much longer."

"Okay. What brings you here?"

"Look, Roy, despite your attitude toward me, I've always admired you, especially your particular talent for getting in and out of houses."

"Roberta, cut the baloney and get to the point."

"An acquaintance of mine has been rude and deceitful to me."

"Which acquaintance?"

"One that's been dishonest, lying and cheating."

"Sounds like the person I'm married to."

"*Roy.*"

"And she be sitting right across from me. Why don't y'all say hello?"

"Damn it, Roy. I'm trying to have a conversation with you, and you're acting like a two-year-old."

"Roberta, the last boyfriend of yours, I shot, got me in a little trouble. You'll have to off Ronnie Harrison yourself."

"Well, I don't want you to shoot Ronnie—at least not yet."

"What do you want me to do in the meantime? Hide in the closet and wait for your boyfriend to stick his hand in your pocketbook again? Because that didn't work out so well the last time. I'm up here doing *your* time."

"You had the wrong attorney. That's why. Then you got yourself a smart woman lawyer like you got a smart wife. That's why I'm here."

"The only reason you're here, Roberta, is for your *own* benefit. So, why don't you pony up, so I can figure out whether or not the bullshit you're selling is worth my time?"

Quieter, leaning in like she was in a confessional booth, "Ronnie Harrison's got a million and a half dollars in his safe at the club right now. More locked up in the basement of his mansion."

"Why're you telling me this?"

"It should concern you."

"Why should it concern me?"

"Roy, someone takes it, Ronnie can't go to the police and say, 'I been robbed of all my undeclared cash,'" looking at Roy to see if the light had turned on.

"Go on."

"Customers at all our clubs gets a twenty-five-percent discount if they use cash, not credit. They spend a thousand dollars, we write up a dupe for say two, three hundred, put that on the books. That's Ronnie's simple but effective trick for making money."

"Which I have no doubt you helped him implement."

"You mean, was it was my idea?"

"Who else's was it?"

"Roy, the question ain't whether we overcharge, but what the customer is willing to pay, and he does."

"And what if the government takes all y'all liquor bills, figure out what y'all really make?"

"It's obvious you don't know squat about business. That's why you're in here."

"You can leave anytime you want, Roberta. Gate's over there," pointing with his phone.

She leaned into the hard separation window. "Listen to me, Roy. End of the month, all the cash is brought to Ronnie's house from all the clubs—Port St. Lucie, Sarasota, Orlando, Miami—before it's moved offshore. And end of the month is end of this week."

"Where offshore?"

Roberta noticed something bright reflecting in the corner of the window. "What's that thing in the guard's hand?"

"For when things get out of hand."

"Is he gonna use it?"

"Not unless you want him to. Where's this boat go?"

"Antigua. Besides tourism, Roy, they love doing laundry. The biggest banker there is our best customer. He's proposed to all the girls and wants to put Julia on the Eastern Caribbean dollar."

"Who's on it now?"

"Queen Elizabeth."

"She know about this?"

"*Who?*"

"The queen."

"Not yet, but the banker's opened accounts for all of us. Says when us girls get rich to stop by, but first we have to hit Ronnie's club. That's the easy one. His mansion—that's another matter."

"I'm not following you."

"Roy, my life hasn't been easy these past five years raising a kid all alone."

"You think mine's been easy?"

"Roy, I'm trying to be serious. Not score points."

"You coulda fooled me."

"You want me to leave, Roy? I can get up and go right now."

"I wouldn't stop you."

"You should. Ronnie Harrison is the most self-absorbed male I've ever met besides you. If you'd been a woman, this whole discussion would have been over by now."

"You still haven't answered my question."

Roberta shed a tear. "I used to eat out every night. Finest of restaurants. I finally met a man who appreciated my talents. Now I go home and eat all alone with a cat."

"Get a dog."

Grabbing a tissue. Patting her eyes. "Roy, there was a time you used to get jealous."

"Look what it got me: time."

"*Roy*, I am still your wife, and I need help."

"What kinda help? Finding a new boyfriend?"

"You're not funny, and you're not listening."

"There's nothing to listen to, Roberta."

"I'm giving you half, Roy. *Half.*"

"Half a what? Heartache?"

Leaning into him. Her chest pressing against the board's edge, "Half the one-point-five million in the office safe and half of whatever's in Ronnie Harrison's safe at the mansion, which I can assure you is seven figures because he's got a shitload of loose diamonds hidden there."

Roy could whisper too. "Then you'll have to do better than that."

"*Better?* When was the last time somebody offered you an easy million dollars?"

"Nothing in life is easy, Roberta. *Nothing.*"

"You don't have a dime to your name. That alone should make it *real* easy."

"Roberta, if you think I'm gonna partner up with you, you can forget it."

"Damn it, Roy. I don't need you. I've already spoken to Lawton."

Not believing her, "What did he say?"

"None of your business."

Roy leaned back. "Thanks for the visit."

"Don't be a fool, Roy."

"Thanks for finally stopping by after five years, Roberta. I really appreciate the wonderful time we had."

"You're still not listening to me, Roy."

"I heard every word you said."

"I will do this alone if I have to."

"Go ahead. Just keep me outta your plans."

"I goddamn will," saying it too loudly. Lowering her voice, "I got Ronnie's codebook for the safes. No safecracking bullshit." Roy, now listening. "And I won't have to worry about splitting anything. I can keep it all to myself."

"But you was just thinking—" Roberta sat back, arms folded, sure that she was now in the driver's seat—"that you'll get me to help you work the combination 'cause you already tried it and had no luck."

Lying, "I never once tried it."

"You tried it before Ronnie threw you outta the house for that new girl, but you couldn't get it to open. Safes can be tricky if you've never worked one before."

"Bullshit. You turn right, left, and right, and left all the way, and then right and left and back."

"But it wouldn't open."

"It should've."

"But it didn't."

"The code could be for another safe. That's why I need your help."

"Roberta—"

"What?"

"I think I know what your problem is."

"What?"

"Besides not knowing what the hell you're doing, you're thinking, should there be any trouble with Ronnie when he finds the money missing, I'll be the one to take the rap since I got a reputation for entering people's houses."

"You wouldn't help me if I was in trouble, Roy?"

"No."

There was a melting down of Roberta's face. She looked short of breath, unsure in her gaze, as if she had just placed all her money on the color red and the roulette wheel struck black. Taking deep breaths, she put her hands flatly against the separation window then hit it. The guard came over. Roy let him know everything was okay. Roberta slipped on her black Versace shades and said as coolly as she could, "I'll be here day of release to pick you up. You'll help me open those safes. Then I don't ever want to see you again." She was gone.

CHAPTER FIVE

Marty Bannister, the head bartender of the Tote Him Pole Gentleman's Club, signed the release for twenty cases of liquor. The delivery guy looked up from his handheld. "Who's the case of Heaven Hill for?"

Marty said to the smarty-pants, "I want a paper receipt."

The delivery guy hit enter. "Roberta said all transactions are now done online and e-mailed directly to her."

"I'm the head bartender of this club, *not* Roberta."

"Sure, Marty. Whatever you say. As long as Roberta gives the okay. By the way," as if he didn't know, "who's the case of Heaven Hill for?"

"Me." One of his perks.

"Well, I don't get cash straight up, no hooch."

Marty was about to give the delivery guy the bird when he saw him lift the case of bourbon into the truck with one hand. Marty had another idea. He headed through the floor-show room to the main office. Roberta wasn't there, so he could talk man-to-man with Ronnie: let him know she was fucking up his business.

Marty zoomed past Roberta's big granite desk and coasted into Ronnie's private office: a large expansive retreat of upholstered white cowhide and state-of-the-art chrome furniture. Ronnie was facing his desk. Pants down to his ankles. Hands over Clarice, one of the pole-dancing girls and new live-in at the mansion. Her tennis skirt pulled up over her fanny. The expression on her face of someone laughing so hard it hurt. Ronnie pointed for Marty to sit down and wait.

Ten minutes later, Ronnie walked out of his office with Clarice adjusting her skirt. Marty said, "Didgya move out all of Roberta's stuff yet?"

Clarice stuck her nose up in the air.

Ronnie said to Marty, "The liquor shipment come in?"

"Yeah," getting up out of Roberta's chair, "I'd like to have a word with you about that." Following Ronnie, "All these years I've had your back. I'm the only person you can trust. It's never been about money, just our deep friendship."

"Get to the point, Marty."

"Roberta."

"What about her?"

"She thinks she's head bartender now."

"You got a problem with Roberta? Take it up with her."

"I can't. She's picking up her husband at Starke today."

"Good."

"You didn't hear me, Ronnie."

"Hear what?"

"It's that prison we talked about. Where Roy LaHood was sent."

"What about it?"

"LaHood's gonna kill you."

"Roberta *told* you that?"

"Didn't have to. She talks trash behind your back all day long."

"Maybe her husband will kill her for cheating on him," lifting his shirt. Showing Marty his new Glock .45 semiautomatic. "He comes after me, I'm prepared," slapping the holster.

"I hope you have better luck than your brother did," seeing fear in Ronnie's face that before wasn't there.

On their way out of the club."I hope you paid for the Heaven Hill, Marty. Otherwise, I'm taking it out of your salary."

Marty followed Ronnie to the parking lot, where the Florida heat was oven hot. "That nigger's gonna kill you, Ronnie, just the way he did Raydel Palmero."

"You steal another ounce of booze from this club, *I'll* kill you."

"You're worried about a case of booze?"

"Roberta is," opening the door to his Mercedes. Patting Clarice's bottom to get in. Leaving Marty in the heat. But not the thought of Roy LaHood.

CHAPTER SIX

Roberta angled her Beamer into the curb about a mile away from Union Correctional Facility at Starke. Roy tapped the passenger window. The door automatically unlocked.

Roy said, "Why so far away?"

"Why so close?" Roberta hit the gas.

Roy grabbed the dashboard with both hands. "You *mind* I shut the door first?"

Roberta was impatient with every vehicle, every light that turned red, every song in her playlist, and when Roy said, "Something bugging you?" she gunned the Beamer.

Roberta hollered, "There's somewhere north of three million dollars sitting in Ronnie Harrison's safes. All of it undeclared cash with a parcel of unset diamonds to boot. You should be jumping all over me to go after it. Instead, you act like you got a trust fund waiting for you in every state."

"I'd like to enjoy my freedom a little while, if ya don't mind." There was a glazed look in his eye Roberta didn't like.

"Roy, the money is undeclared cash. Ronnie can't report it as stolen since it's already been stolen. You want to enjoy your freedom? This is the road to it."

"You take down someone, it's never easy. Stuff always happens."

"Ronnie's a moron. He acts tough, but he isn't."

"He seems to have done all right for himself."

"With *me* in charge. I'm not saying he's completely dumb, Roy, but he's always two sandwiches short of a picnic, and if he's not eating, he's watering his plants. If he's not taking a dump, he's counting his money. If he's not sleeping, he's fornicating."

"Roberta, you seen all this money?"

"*Every* night. I leave the receipts in a safety box locked at the bottom of my desk. Then I turn the alarm on and leave. End of the week, Ronnie opens the big safe and puts in what's collected from all over. End of the month, he takes it all out to his mansion and sails it offshore to Antigua and then hands it over to a banker who's one of our best customers. It's routine. Scheduled. Synched. Everything in his life from walking his dog, watering his petunias, collecting cash, getting laid, and taking a dump is synchronized."

"I do believe there's more to a man than that."

"Geezuz, that's what I used to think," giving Roy the cold stare as she pulled something out of her pocketbook. "Here's the key to our future," waving it in his face. "You wanna work Walmart or live in a dream house by the ocean? Play golf in the afternoon or schlep cartons of diapers down endless aisles?" Looking at Roy. Hoping he was listening. "You can't even compare the one to the other," wondering if he could.

Roy said, "You *sure* about the money?"

"Take a *long* look at this," holding up the blue booklet. "This here is Ronnie's codebook to his safes. He used to hide it in his basement, but the maid stumbled upon it and thought it belonged somewhere else. He freaked out and spent days looking for it. I told him, 'If this damn booklet is so important, you better let me help you find it, or somebody else will.' I finally found it in Ronnie's gardening box stuck in a Wells Lamont glove of all places. I said, 'Ronnie, you told me this was a booklet of your family's birthdays. Well, there's a whole mess of numbers here, but no birthdays.' I swear; he hissed like a cat."

Roy, eyeing the booklet. "This got the numbers to both safes?"

"Unless your ability to think has been compromised by all that pruno you been drinking in lockup, that's what it is, but it's meaningless if all you want to do is sit on your rear end and stare out in space. What's happened to you, anyway, since I last saw you? They give you some kinda drug to slow you down day of release?"

Roy sat back and shut his eyes. "I'm in love."

Roberta swerved the car back into her lane. "You mind telling me who it is this time?"

Roy spoke the word like powder off his tongue: "Audrey."

"Audrey? You don't mean *Audrey* Audrey?"

"There ain't no other."

"Lawton know anything about this?"

Roy said, "She was gonna come pick me up until you butted in. Now I gotta wait till seven o'clock to see her."

Roberta warned him, "Well, whatever your plans was for tonight, you can forget'em."

"Why?"

"Because I'm taking you somewhere."

"Where?"

"Somewhere we can talk."

"You mean home?

"Roy, you forget. You ain't got a home."

Roberta pulled into the driveway of her house, which was a modest three-bedroom 1930s white Mediterranean with tall French windows Roy had installed under Roberta's expansion plan, which included a garden where a lonely palm tree and some bored petunias were waiting to get robbed.

Roberta, already in the kitchen, put the Chinese takeout and beer on the counter. Roy popped a can and took a walk down memory lane. The first thing he noticed in the living room was that his family's photos were no longer on the wall. He ducked into the dining room and returned to the kitchen. Roberta said, "How was memory lane?"

"Where's all the pictures of my family?"

Roberta had more important things to do than talk about cousins. She gave him his plate of chow mein, couple of noodles tossed on top, chopsticks, and told him, "Sit in the living room. Use the placemats. Don't put your feet up. Use the napkins, *not* the couch." She handed him another two beers.

Roy went into the living room, this time assessing what had been removed: The photo of him in his Clarksdale Wildcats football uniform: one knee on the ground, the other up with his helmet resting on it. A photo of Granny Clementine in her bean yard off Dog Bogg Road. One of Granddaddy Beau LaHood standing by *The 20th Century Limited* in Grand Central Terminal, the train that he had served on as a Pullman porter back in the Jazz Age. But the most hurtful vacancy was the photo of Crystal on his lap her first Christmas: Roy dressed up as Santa, she as a little Santa Cutie.

"You looking for something?"

Roy eased himself around and said to the sweet vision standing in front of him, "You just gonna stand there?"

Crystal ran up and hugged her daddy, both feet off the ground. She kissed him so hard on the cheek he could feel it on the other.

"How's my little girl?"

They sat down on the couch, Crystal, one arm over his shoulder so she could lean up against him.

"How're you, daddy?"

Stand Your Ground

"Couldn't be better with you in my arms."

"Me too," and kissed him again.

"Wasn't a minute I didn't think of you, baby doll."

"I thought of you every day, Daddy, especially when Mama got on my nerves. I told her if you was here, life would be so much better."

"Mama been bad to you?"

"Oh, you don't wanna know how bad, Daddy."

"She do something to hurt my baby?"

"I'm her slave, Daddy. All the time. Minute I take a rest, she's on me to do something else."

"Well, we'll have to fix that."

"You better or I'll go crazy."

"We can't have you do that."

"I gotta move in with you, Daddy. Right now. If we have to live on the street and beg, I'll do it with pride."

"You ain't living on no street."

"Daddy, you don't know how I can't stand that woman. I wanna go to New York City. I've made a name for myself in school with my choreography, and there ain't nothing like having a name. I'm ready for the big time, now, and no one, including you, will get in my way."

"I understand, baby, but dreams can get you a whole lot of trouble if they ain't thought through. Now, I fully understand why you want things so bad you can't wait. But things just don't come 'cause of you wanting them. Sometimes you gotta wait awful long."

"If I stay here, I'll go nuts, Daddy. I don't get my freedom from Mama, I just might lose my mind and never recover."

"Baby doll, freedom is not something you get; it's something you earn."

"I don't care. I want it *now*."

"Look, child. I just got back. I'll take care of all your dreams and make 'em come true, but one step at a time."

"You gonna get your own place?"

"I reckon sooner than later, child."

"I know you got money hidden away."

"Who told you that?"

"Julia."

"Crystal, Julia's just a kid, and kids are apt to a lot of exaggeration."

"Daddy, you haven't seen Julia in a long time. She ain't no kid. She's valedictorian. Aced her math SATs. She's not only a genius, she's the best surfer on the coast and the most beautiful girl in the world. And when she walks down the street, everyone stops and stares. There ain't nothing she can't do and nobody who can challenge her, because she got this power and it radiates like heat. I swear, when she talks to God, he stops everything, and if the devil interrupts, he says sorry faster than the flames that burn around him. But Julia's pissed at you, and it makes me think maybe you haven't been telling me all the truth, because Julia would never lie to me because we're best of friends till death."

"Don't you listen to her. Be your own person."

"I am my own person, daddy, but Julia's tough as nails and true to herself and won't budge for nobody. So you better be careful. All I gotta do is mention your name, and it's like the sun hides and the sky goes dark."

Roy said, "What exactly did she tell you?"

"Told me you got money hidden from when you and Lawton took down that billionairess Wall Street woman, Mrs. Johnson. That's who I took Lawton to see when he got out of Starke. He's living with her now."

"Well, I'm sorry to say this, Crystal, but the money was long gone before I was sent up. Not that I wanted it to happen, but the things I was working on—well, they just didn't work out. So, I'm sorry, but I'll get it all back." He turned to the wall where his family photos should have been. "When did your mama take down my pictures?"

"Soon as you was sent up."

Roberta walked in and handed Crystal a plate of steamed vegetables and chicken.

Crystal said, "I asked for fried rice and an egg roll. Not that."

"You want garbage? Eat from the trash can."

Crystal got up and left the room.

Roberta hollered, "Get back here, girl." Crystal ignored her.

Roy said, "Why do you talk to her like that?"

"Because she won't listen."

"Maybe you don't know how to talk to her."

"You spend five years in a prison, now you're an expert on raising children?"

Roy didn't bother to answer. The digital clock on the cable box said 9:00 p.m. Audrey had said to him, *I'll have something on the stove ready by seven.* He was two hours late. Roy got up and said to Roberta, "I gotta go make a call."

"Who ya calling?"

"That's my business."

"Not if it's on my phone."

"Roberta, all I'm doing is taking two minutes out of your life."

"You can see Audrey tomorrow."

Roy took the phone off the coffee table. "You telling me when I can see somebody?"

"Give me the phone, Roy."

"Roberta, it'll take just two minutes."

Hand stretched out, "*Give* me the phone, Roy."

"You think I can't get my own phone?"

"You're broke. All you got is me. Don't forget that, Roy." Roberta took the phone from him and then leaned back on the sofa. She pointed to the soft chair by her side. "Sit down." Roy took the chair. "I want you to read the numbers in that booklet and tell me the correct combination to the safes. And remember, Roy: you can't get to them without me because I got the club's security system in my head." She reached for the pad and pencil on the coffee table, licked the lead, and waited.

Roy said, "Alarms can be disabled."

"If there's money missing, I'll be on the phone telling the police, 'The person y'all're looking for is Afro American. Six feet six inches tall. And to save y'all time, his name is Roy LaHood, just out of Starke.'"

"They'll want to know how you know all this."

"I'll tell 'em he's married to me and was asking all about the money where I work. Enough for 'em to get interested and enough to keep me in the clear. Now about these numbers. There's up to ten thousand ways to open Ronnie's two safes. I know that because I already spoke to someone who knows such things."

"Why didn't you get him to open it?"

Roberta looked at Roy the way a traffic cop does when he asks for your license and registration. "Just tell me what I want to know, Roy."

Roy picked up the codebook and studied the numbers.

Roberta said, "How do I open the safe?"

"I'll have to sit with it."

Roberta reached over and took the codebook out of his hands. "You can't fool me. You're trying to memorize the numbers."

Tired of getting bossed around, Roy got up. "You need to chill out."

"Roy, either you can open the safe or not. Which is it?"

"Give me the phone."

"Answer my question."

"Let me have the keys to the car."

Giving him a pencil and paper. "Write down the order of the numbers and how to turn the combination."

Roy took the booklet and wrote out whatever came to his head.

Roberta said, "I'm going to test this out first thing in the morning. Then maybe you can get to use the car."

"I want the keys now, Roberta."

"You sit down and finish your meal. You've had a long day. I suggest you take a shower, watch some TV. Then we'll get up early, and I'll decide what we'll do next."

Roy leaned over Roberta and her plate of curried pineapple chicken. She was looking right up at him with more than a little fear in her eyes. "*Give* me the keys, Roberta."

"Roy. *Sit* down. I don't like your attitude."

"I can take the keys from you if I want."

Hiding the keys under her behind. "Roy, you couldn't get a job at McDonald's."

Breathing hard on her. "I can get a job anywhere. My record has been cleared."

"All they have to do is look you up. Nobody's gonna hire the infamous Four-Minute Burglar."

It would have been very easy to lift Roberta up, turn her face-down on the couch, and take the keys. The hard part would've been afterward. The next day. The day after. Roberta liked revenge the way mosquitoes like blood. He went down the hall and knocked on Crystal's door. "I need a few dollars, baby doll. I gotta get somewhere fast."

Crystal at the door. "I'm going out now. Meet me on East Crescent in ten minutes. I'll take you where you want."

"Thank you, baby."

Roberta, nose to the door. "What's going on here?" She moved past Roy and into Crystal's room. "What the hell did he say to you, Crystal?"

"Daddy said he loves me."

Roy was already past the living room. Roberta catching up. "Get back inside this house, Roy, if you know what's good for you." She hollered out into the street, "You wanna sleep in the gutter, Roy? That's where you'll sleep. That's where you'll sleep *every* night." Then he got pelted. "Go ahead, ya big loser. You're forty-six years old. Can't even support your kid. *I* have to. *I* pay the bills. *I* do everything for everyone, and what do *I* get? Nothing. Even Ronnie Harrison can't fire me. No one can. I'm too fucking good."

One of the neighbors chimed in, "Welcome back, Roy."

Twenty minutes later Crystal pulled up on East Crescent. Roy got in the cab of the Raptor the way a package lands: hard and with a thud. He said, "When you get home later, I want you to do me a very special favor."

"I'll do anything you want, Daddy."

"Find me a blue booklet your mama has and bring it to me."

"A *what?*"

"A slim blue booklet."

"Why?"

"You want your freedom?"

She hit the gas pedal. "You'll have it tomorrow."

CHAPTER SEVEN

The palm tree off the side of Audrey Gibbs's Jensen Beach Surfside Bungalow Colony cast a long morning shadow over Gertie Eccles, who was fast asleep on a lounge chair with a little Chihuahua, named Handsome, tucked between her legs. Audrey turned her gaze from the kitchen window and said in a drawl as soft as the breeze off the ocean, "Funny how that old lady always naps toward my bungalow like she's listening in."

Crystal, at the other end of the line, "You mean crazy old Gertie?"

"Crazy ain't the half of it. So what happened when y'all got there?"

"Lawton got whisked away. But I can tell you he's not in love with that old billionaire lady at all."

"That's his problem."

"All he did was talk about you."

"He can talk all he wants," Audrey said. "Julia and I are jumping later. You coming along?"

"Sure, but Lawton said he'd give up all her fortune if he could just have you back."

"He'd better hold onto her money."

"Audrey, I don't mean to be nosey, but are you in love with my father?"

"Who said I'm in love with him?"

"*He* did."

"Your father's an old friend. That's how I love him."

"He thinks otherwise."

"Thanks for the gossip, Crystal, but I gotta earn a few dollars this morning at the pool teaching the kids."

"Audrey."

"What?"

"He was so sad."

"Who?"

"Lawton."

"A man makes his own sadness," and hung up.

Gertie Eccles was gone. Her sun visor and slippers were still by the lounge chair, as well as Handsome, whose nose was pointing anxiously toward her bungalow. Audrey was worried, not for Gertie, but for old Uncle Herb, Gertie's boyfriend, who hadn't been feeling well. Audrey always looked forward to when he'd walk over, sit down with a bottle of pear schnapps, and tell her about the old days in New York's Lower East Side, with all its miracles and disasters, plagues and calamities, deaths and misfortunes that seemed to accumulate and vanish faster than the time went by telling it. Old Herb would say New York is still a place to make a fortune, his nephew Bobby Braren being an example: the real-estate maven, movie producer, conceptual-art collector, meticulous womanizer who culled the rosters of Soho, Tribeca, and the West Village for love, but with the recent financial collapse, disappearing middle class, and rampant gun violence, he was going to use art to change the world. Bring people together. And if he couldn't create the art that would shame the world to its senses, then he would buy it and shame everyone else for not owning it. Herb would point his cigar at Audrey, roll his eyes, and say, *Oiy!* as if the boy had gone mad. Gertie, a pigeon at picking up pieces of information, would nudge Audrey whenever Uncle Herb turned to spit into his handkerchief. "I told Bobby all about ya, Audrey. Said he can't wait to jump the broom. You'll love New York City with all Bobby's money."

New York City. Audrey wasn't too sure about the Big Apple. She'd never been there, but there was this old movie that scared the hell out of her where the main character, taxi driver Travis Bickle, cruises dark and dirty 1970s Manhattan. Its gravity sucking up its citizens like a swamp and then turning them into slow-moving waste. This strange island of concrete, glass, and asphalt, where dreams are taken out at night and collected like trash in the morning. Could an apple even grow there? Audrey had been told things had changed for the better since that movie had been made. The boom, before the financial collapse of '08, had slicked up the place, and the revamped police department had cleaned up the crime, but Audrey wasn't so sure. She knew how things could be covered up. Travis Bickle could now be a passenger in a taxi from Wall Street, or maybe in an Uber.

Gertie Eccles was back in her lounge chair as if nothing had happened. Old Herb was wheezing in the yard. He sounded like an old motor starting up and then dying out. He spent most of the day sitting in a lounge chair outside or in his Big Boy, inside, dozing. A newspaper always on his lap, unread. Children, running by, would wake him up for a moment; then like a light, he'd go out again. He lived by the hour and slept by the week.

Audrey's bungalow door opened. A voice, deep and dry, like smoke from a match, filled the room. "It's been a while."

She reached for the coffeemaker. Poured two cups. Black for her, black two sugars for the man just out of prison. He took the coffee and said, "You remember how I like it." Curious about the nipple jewelry. Audrey was wearing nothing else but a lace thong; she hadn't been expecting visitors.

"What happened last night?"

Roy said, "I ended up sleeping on the beach."

"Roberta's called a hundred times this morning."

"She can go to hell."

"What happened with y'all?"

Roy moved his eyes off her full breasts to the untanned shoulder stripes that divided her lean shoulders. He said, "Roberta is paranoid. Always thinks the whole world is out to get her." He watched the thin, long gold chain sway as Audrey leaned in with a slice of Lady Baltimore cake.

She said, "If I know Roberta, it had to do with money."

Roy stared at the beautiful forty-year-old Audrey, her quiet but determined face a constant sorrow. "I like the jewelry."

"A client of mine from the club."

"Gave it to you?"

"Owns one of those shops. Said I could have anything I want."

"Something you been thinking about?"

"No. He showed it to me. Tried it on. Thought it was interesting."

She kept an eye on Roy as he walked over to the refrigerator and opened the freezer. "I'm dying for some ice cream. It's been years," and pulled out a big tub of rocky road. "I may need a place to stay for a night or so, if it's all right with you."

"Roberta threw you out already?"

"I walked out," looking for a spoon. "Where's Julia?"

"Giving a surfing lesson on the beach."

"Works hard that little girl."

"She's not little anymore, Roy."

"Crystal been telling me y'all jump together."

"We have fun when we can."

"Don't forget who taught you."

Smiling, "Don't worry." Seeing Roy and Lawton in their Ranger uniforms. Sergeant LaHood. Sergeant Gibbs. The combat badges. Ranger parachutist badges. Men good at what they did.

"Look, I been thinking, and I just can't hold onto what I feel no longer. All them letters you wrote me."

"I hope they soothed you, Roy."

"They did more than that."

"You're eating all of Julia's ice cream."

Checking the tub. "Got her name on it?"

"Does it have yours?"

"I'm just taking a bite."

"She'll take a bite out of you."

Laughing, "Little Julia?" Seeing her in his mind. The little blond girl who rode the waves on his shoulders. Cried when a big one crushed her. "Hell, I used to wipe her tears away when she got a boo-boo," approaching Audrey, his voice tender. "I just want to be honest with you."

"Don't."

"Audrey."

"I'm not interested."

"I love you."

Audrey got up from the table and put on a T-shirt from the laundry basket.

Roy said, "Am I a fool for saying that?"

"We're all fools."

Coming to her, "Audrey."

"*Don't.*"

"I do believe on some level you feel the same way as I do."

"Roy, you confuse friendship with romance," and moved away from him.

The wind pushed up against the back screen door. In the distance, a girl in a yellow-and-black two-piece sunk her feet into the deep, hot sand. A surfboard under one arm. Her long blond hair whipping in the wind. She sculpted the space around her, improving every inch she walked. Her eyes, even at a distance, were compelling, complex, and determined. She crossed through the small patio, leaned her board against the bungalow, and entered through the backdoor. A puddle grew at her feet. "Who's he?" Julia didn't look at Roy as much as dismiss him.

Audrey said, "You remember Roy."

"That's my ice cream."

Roy offered her the tub. "My have you grown," the shock on his face hard to hide.

Holding the empty tub. "There's nothing left."

"I'll get you some more."

Julia went to the kitchen and tossed it in the trash can.

Audrey said, "I left your college material on the table." She took her gear off the laundry rack. "I'm late. I've got to get to the pool. Roy will be staying with us for a while."

"This place is small enough without him."

"I didn't say forever." Audrey, on her way out. "I'll be back by noon. Crystal will pick us up." Riding off on her Ducati Monster.

Roy and Julia were left alone to stare at each other like strangers in the middle of nowhere. Julia, five-four, was not the least intimidated by the six-feet-six man. "Why aren't you at *your* house?"

"I'm here."

Julia poured herself coffee and then turned around and leaned against the counter. "You mean you got kicked outta your house."

"You could say that."

Roy walked toward her.

Julia said, "Where ya going?"

"I'd like some more coffee."

"Put a dollar down."

"You gotta be kidding?"

Julia blocked the coffee machine.

Roy said, "Look, I know what's bugging you, but you got it all wrong."

"Ya think so?"

"Yeah."

"Ya still want coffee?"

"Sure."

"Put two dollars down."

"And I thought Roberta was a pain."

"You're the dummy who married her."

"You're the dummy who works for her."

"You're so damn smart, you spent a half a million dollars of my father's cut on hotels, whores, liquor, surfing, boating, golfing, and left my mother and me with nothing."

"I'm sorry."

"You're *sorry*?"

Avoiding her stare. "I heard you aced your SATs."

"So what?"

"Valedictorian."

"You're gonna gimme a medal?"

"If there was one, I would."

"I'd give it right back."

Roy said, "Your mama teach you to be like that?"

"Like what?"

"Ornery."

"Life teaches me that."

"Your mama's not angry with me."

"She hates you."

"Then why did she let me in here?"

"She didn't let you in here. You walked in."

"Your mama invited me."

"She made a mistake."

"I don't like your tone of voice."

"*Leave.*"

"You don't understand."

"*I* don't understand?"

"Look, that crazy old rich lady went and fell in love with your father, so we used that to our advantage, but it was our trust of you and your mother that we relied on to get us through."

"You mean the trust of *you*. My father got you off the hook and out of jail for complicity in the hiest. Then you went and spent his cut."

Roy said, "I invested it." Shrugging. "Didn't work out. That's all."

"*Didn't work out.*" Grabbing a sarong beach cover-up. "And stop looking at my legs. That's all you've doing since I walked in."

Roy was thinking Julia had that quality so few women had: the ability to make a man, within seconds of seeing her, feel hopeless unless he could have her, no matter how bad her attitude was. Roy said, "You may have forgotten, but we used to be real good friends. I'd just like us not to forget all the good times we had when you was a kid."

"I'm not a kid."

"I remember the day you was born."

"I don't."

"What I'm saying is, we go back a long way."

"I don't care we go back to the goddamn moon."

"What's your problem, Julia?"

"*You're* my problem."

"Give me a few days."

"For *what?*"

"For what I have to do."

"*What's* that?"

"Getting what I owe y'all."

Pointing to him as if drawing blood. "You *better.*"

Taking a step toward Julia. "Don't threaten me."

"You think I like dancing in a fuck joint?"

"Your mama and I already spoke about that."
"*You* and I haven't."
"I'll make it up to you."
"Like you make everything up."
"You got a bad attitude, girl."
"You're in *my* home."
"Then treat me as a guest."
"You're not a guest. You're a freeloader. *Get out.*"

Roy headed to the door. He wanted the codebook to Ronnie Harrison's safes now more than ever.

CHAPTER EIGHT

Roberta emptied all the drawers. Then the closets. She checked her clothing from the night before. The day before. The month before. She checked the living room, kitchen. Her Beamer. The floorboard. Behind the visor. Under the driver's seat. All the seats. In the trunk. She went back inside the house and checked under all the furniture. Her bed. In her bed. The night table. Under it. Around it. Inside it. She jammed her toe on the bedpost and went reeling back. Nothing stopped her. She stayed nose down to the floor. Searched the entire house on her chin until the last wall was up against her head and the lint deep into her nails. Then she heard the kitchen door open. Roberta hobbled toward it.

Crystal took a pound of coffee out of a bag and said to her mother, "You forgot to go shopping yesterday." She plunked the can on the counter. Popped the cover. Placed a filter in the Bonavita. Poured in the grounds. Hit the button. Walked around her mother.

Roberta hissed, "You got two seconds to return my booklet."

Crystal said, "If you're looking for your vibrator, it's in your bed."

Roberta lost her balance as she swung her arm off her sore right foot. She fell back in a zigzag and hit her head on the kitchen stove and landed on the floor like the roof had collapsed. Instead of a scream, there was a numbness that choked the air. She was thinking: The booklet. The money. That son of a bitch Roy. Then she heard the Raptor turn the corner. Crystal was never coming back.

CHAPTER NINE

The Jupiter Dunes eighteenth green, with its undulating surface, steep approach, and squid-shaped bunker lurking to the right, made Roy feel as if he were about to get swallowed up. The late summer sun had already scorched the grass, and Roy was feeling the heat as he made his putt for birdie.

Lawton, standing on the other side of the pin, watched the ball roll just short of the cup. "Roy, you owe me a sawbuck."

"That ball is *in*."

"I don't play gimmes, Roy, like everybody else. I score every shot. The golf ball is on the lip of the cup, *not* in it."

Roy pulled out his meager roll and peeled off a ten. "If the damn groundskeeper mowed the green right, there'd be no rising edge on my side of the cup. I tied you and you know it."

"That's why I love playing with you and everybody else, Roy. Y'all prove to me time and again people are born liars."

"I'm rusty. That's all. And that ain't a lie." They headed to the car. "You made up your mind about the job?"

"I just spent ten years in a prison. I don't plan on going back."

"Lawton, this heist is like stealing candy from a baby. I got the codebook right here with the numbers. Crystal knows the security layout. You want something easier? Tell me what is."

"Nothing's easy, Roy. You know that better than I do."

"Yeah, but what if the gig with the old lady don't pan out?"

They reached Mrs. Johnson's Bentley, which Lawton had borrowed for the outing.

"So far it's going all right."

"*So far* ain't even a week, Lawton. There's upward of three million dollars stashed in the club and at Ronnie Harrison's Sailfish Point mansion. Plus a velvet bag of loose diamonds. More than enough to pay off what I owe you from the last job and get Julia off my ass."

"Could also be nothing."

"Lawton, your negativity's working against you. How often does somebody drop their codebook in your lap? This ain't a top-drawer job. It's the whole kit and caboodle. You take Ronnie Harrison's club while I take down the house. Fifty-fifty cut as usual."

"Which place has more money?"

"Don't matter. Whatever we take, we split. We're talking around three million dollars, or Roberta wouldn't be so riled up."

"How does she fit into the cut, Roy?"

"She don't."

"She know that?"

"The less she knows, the better."

They got into the motorized man cave that mainlined luxury quicker than a syringe and drove off. Roy smoothed his hand over the leather dashboard. "We'll be able to buy one of these in a few days."

"I already have one."

"It ain't yours, Lawton."

"Roy, why buy a Bentley when you can use one for nothing?"

Ten minutes later they pulled into the Johnson estate on Jupiter Island. Roy stared out the window and almost wept at the dreamlike expanse of land right off the Atlantic Ocean. He said, "Imagine the old lady was thirty-five, not seventy-five."

Lawton said, "I been doing that the moment I walked outta prison."

Mrs. Johnson escorted her two guests to the garden just off the ocean, which sparkled as brightly as uncorked Champagne. They were seated by Clemens, the butler, at a luncheon table that had lilies pouring out of vases and polished silverware glinting in the sun. Two other servants appeared: Silent and Thorough. They were equipped with white coats, black ties, and black trousers. *Yes, sir* and *No, sir* were the extent of their vocabulary. Their ability to navigate a table and serve was as seamless as a skater doing figure eights. One poured wine as if from a fountain; the other refilled like Elijah.

Mrs. Johnson was seated at the head of the table. The boys, on either side. She said, "Y'all must be hungry, so don't be polite."

Roy grabbed a sandwich from the silver tray. He carefully set it on his plate and delicately withdrew a yellow-frilled toothpick as if a fuse had been planted underneath. Lawton waited to be served. The wine was a Bouchard Pere et Fils Chablis '05. Crisp and chilled.

Mrs. Johnson said, "We're all starting a new life. May it be kinder than the last one."

They clinked glasses and grinned like socialites at a Hamptons or Nantucket summer lawn party where whimsical feats are celebrated and small gestures are taken as grand impressions. Mrs. Johnson, epic in haute couture, might have appeared dainty to the untrained eye, but a butter knife she wasn't. She had talons hidden beneath a beauty that hadn't vanished as much as retreated. Her strawberry-blond hair of youth was now brittle after years of coloring. Her milky skin cast a lardy sheen that creased and sagged at the neck, but glossed whenever she leaned into the sun; and like a banking aircraft, her lines, frayed of age and the injury of time, momentarily disappeared; but it was her eyes that prompted Roy to stare whenever he thought she wasn't looking. They were inviting and mindful and, like Julia's, had a fierceness and trip wire ready to snap. Mrs. Johnson, aware of Roy's interest, crossed her legs. They went lean and long. He thought she had an old-school sexiness that was grateful for attention and a new-school ardor that showed passion was still left in the old mare; and though one of them was getting older and getting used to the idea, the other was used to it and getting impatient with the notion that having sex with her was a Socratic experience—but then a debate does have its heated moments.

Mrs. Johnson finished another glass of wine. The alcohol made it easier for her to reach deeper into her mind. "Too many men in my life have had little use for my ideas. If you hadn't earned money, you didn't know hoot. But I was raised with the best of everything and knew how to edit the winners and losers from my life. My friends were those whom I chose. Some were poets, mostly bad ones; they had the best of hearts but the dullest quills. Others were hunters that hunted on a full stomach. Then there were the businessmen and politicians who dispatched their enemies after porterhouses and cigars. The same went for all the engineers, teachers, sailors, and characters in the books that I have loved or hated. All were cruel. All selfish, but those who had a sense of humor I befriended, despite their list of crimes. And I can assure you, they will be the last echo heard when this universe—or should I say, madness—expires. In the meantime, we live like crabs and grip the sand looking for mates in whatever way we can. Regardless, I have never loved a man who wasn't sooner or later less than what he had sold me, less than what I had originally loved, and worse, less than I what I had so foolishly imagined.

I've been so disappointed in love that I no longer care. No longer worry. No longer demand any level of perfection. Instead, I hunger for truancy, excitement, someone with whom I can talk. A true companion. For we all live for one thing and one thing only, and that is to be free from the bounds and limitations of earth and its one oppressive chain: time." Turning to Roy, "It is for these reasons that I have accepted Lawton's offer of marriage, but I warn anyone who thinks I'm a fool: I am not. I know men and the ways of the world. My last husband, Leyland, was punctual in all his affairs. A man with career, substance, national prominence, dependability, and one with whom I believed I could plan and execute life on a grander scale. We plotted the governor's office, a possible Senate run, even the White House. We talked economics, infrastructure, national debt, civil service, educational reform, innovation, wars to avoid and fight. Art to support, or better yet invest. Policies to reverse. New ones to implement and old ones to subvert. But most of all, the people to elevate to our inner circle and those to destroy who threatened it. Yet no matter how much power we acquired, there were always others hungrily chumming nearby. So, with all our achievements, we ended up in a world just as miserable as the one we had entered: making deals to stay alive; keeping necessary associations with vile, duplicitous people to maintain status and success. I thought we could bring change to this world, but Leyland was content to leave it the way he had found it. Then—I lost Ellen: my only child. I quickly fell into a darkness of mind that locked me out of each day, until one night, alone in my room, a stranger's voice said, 'It will be even lonelier if you take your life.'"

Mrs. Johnson turned to Lawton and raised her glass, but it was like lifting a sword over someone already dead. She stared into space. At what? Lawton wasn't sure. Roy didn't care. They took dessert and then a tour of the estate.

CHAPTER TEN

That evening Audrey was cleaning the lint screen of the community dryer when her phone rang. A dull demotic voice materialized. "Why don't you come on up?"

Audrey slipped the lint screen back in. "Who is this?"

"It's a beautiful night. Why don't we take a little ride in my dinghy."

"*Who* is this?"

"Ronnie."

Audrey, more than surprised. "Ronnie Harrison?"

"Yeah. Come on up to the mansion."

"You're sure you got the right number, Ronnie?"

"Sure, I'm sure. It's about business."

"I can't, Ronnie. I'm doing laundry."

"When you're done."

"It won't be done for an hour."

"Forget about the laundry."

"I'm not dressed."

"Neither am I."

"I'm a mess."

"Who isn't?"

"I really can't, Ronnie."

"The evening's early."

"Why tonight?"

Ronnie, now the boss. "Because I said so. Here are the directions—"

Unlike the club's young dancers, Audrey had never been invited to Ronnie Harrison's Sailfish Point waterfront mansion. Roberta had told her she was too old to hang around a pool with a bunch of twenty-year-olds: "It would be like having your mother there."

Clarice, on the other hand, made it a point of telling Audrey that not only was Julia an overrated dancer and beauty, but that she, Clarice, had been invited to the mansion several times. "And the only way to walk down the stairway of Ronnie's multimillion dollar shack is to approach it like a jet on a runway and take off," her nose up in the air. "And you get banana pancakes for breakfast if you stay over."

Audrey said, "How many did you eat?"

Clarice wouldn't tell.

Ten o'clock, Ronnie's black miniature schnauzer went into a rage as Audrey walked through the flow of lights from garage number two. Ronnie shooed the dog inside and said, "I got over a hundred fifty different outdoor plants have to be watered every three days. People I pay do ten then say fuck it and leave. I got these flowers in the front to finish; then we can go inside and have some fun." He gazed at her old model Ducati Monster she had picked up on Craigslist. "How was your ride?"

Audrey thought her boss looked funny holding a cognac glass big enough for a goldfish to do laps. He wore white high-tops, tennis shorts from the days of Pancho Gonzalez, and a worn-out Duke

T-shirt: blue block letters stamped over gray. Ronnie looked more like the gardener.

Audrey said, "The ride was fine."

"We never talk much. Do we?"

"I don't think we've ever really talked."

Ronnie tweaked one of the blue iris stalks. "You need to freshen up?"

"I'm fine."

"A drink?"

"Not thirsty."

"I meant something else."

"No."

Then pointing the water can at her good lean legs. "You always wear sundresses?"

"Not always."

Ronnie moved to the next plant. "Do me a favor. Bring me the hose. It's over there."

Audrey brought him the hose that was in the dirt by the bushes.

Ronnie said, "You gotta turn it on first."

She walked over to the bibcock by the side of the library room and bent over. Ronnie started at her ankles then worked his way up. Audrey kept her hand on the back of her sundress to let him know she wasn't dumb.

She said, "Now what?"

"Put the hose in the can for me."

They stood side by side as it filled up.

Ronnie said, "I like your ride." Then he nudged Audrey to look at garage number five, where a spanking-new matte-black Ducati Monster 1200 S was parked deep to the side of a two-tone Wave Runner. It was just like Audrey's, except hers was ten years old with a short-tail kit already installed.

Ronnie, staring at her groin. "Girl wears a sundress on a motorcycle is taking a chance."

"Not if you tuck it under." Audrey pointed to Ronnie's new bike. "How come you never ride it to work?"

"I just got it. Saw yours in the lot. Had to have one."

She said, "You wanna go for a ride?"

"I gotta get a license first."

"You don't have a license?"

"You don't need a license to buy a bike."

"You don't need one to ride one."

"It's taking a chance riding without a license," Ronnie said.

"You think the police will know?"

"Somehow, I think they know when you don't have a license. You have a license?"

"Twenty-two years."

"Maybe you could give me a lesson," Ronnie said. "My bike kind of jumps out on me, if you know what I mean."

"You're supposed to know how to ride if you buy a 1200 S."

Ronnie took the insult as part of getting to know each other. He straightened another pesky blue iris thinking Audrey might be hitting forty, but she was gliding in, not crashing. He walked over to the hose line and wrapped it around its wagon; then he went to the front door, where his schnauzer was on its paws ready to start squawking.

Audrey said, "Does Clarice know I'm here?"

"No."

"You didn't bring me here to teach you how to ride a motorcycle?"

Changing his mind about going inside. "You eat supper?"

"Why?"

"There's a clam shack down 1A. Come dressed as you are. Right on the beach."

Audrey wondered, "Is Clarice coming?"

Ronnie, closer. "She's visiting her mother tonight."

Stepping away from him. "So, you thought you'd call me?"

Putting a hand on Audrey's shoulder.

Audrey, pushing it away. "What happened between you and Roberta?"

"Roberta's a handful."

"You're not?"

"Picking on me already?"

"I'm not too sure what you mean by 'already,'" still annoyed that he had touched her.

"Why don't we have some dinner? Talk. It's a beautiful evening."

"I thought you wanted to talk to me about business."

"I do," Ronnie said, "but this is not the place."

Audrey pulled her bike out of the garage and swung her leg over the saddle. She switched on the ignition. "You think you can handle piggyback?"

Audrey had to move Ronnie's hands now and then to let him know he was getting frisky. She took the Monster up to ninety, so he'd get the message. He did when she turned flat on a corner. Fifteen minutes later Ronnie was sitting safely in a fixed chair facing the ocean with a bottle of chenin blanc planted on his side of the table. The first two pours were for him. The third, he reached over. Audrey covered her glass. "I don't drink and ride."

"You mean drink and drive."

"What's the difference?"

"I was making a joke."

The waitress put a basket of hot garlic bread on the table with a complimentary bottle of sparkling water. Audrey stared at the girl. Julia's age. Blond. Blue eyed. No tattoos. A ponytail. Trendy prescription glasses. A T-shirt that said "Blue Devil Pride." And an all-American smile.

Audrey said to her, "What's a Blue Devil?"

Handing them menus. "I go to Duke."

Ronnie pointed to his T-shirt: the big "DUKE" in blue.

Audrey was thinking about the new dolphin tattoo inked on Julia's rear end below the tramp stamp that had been inked a month before. Audrey had said to Julia, "Your backside's getting a bit crowded." Julia reminded her, "So is this house, Mama."

Ronnie ordered for them. "You're not in a good mood, are you?"

Audrey said, "I don't mean to be blunt, but all the time I've been working at your club, you don't even say hello. Now the royal treatment. Why?"

Ronnie dunked his bread in the dip. "I might be needing another bookkeeper."

"Why?"

"Roberta still has her job. But I might be opening another new place out of state. So I'll need someone with experience. Someone I know who can hold the fort." Leaning into Audrey. "This is about moving up in the organization."

"I don't understand."

"What don't you understand?"

"Moving up in the organization."

"I need someone the girls can look up to. Mother figure."

"What about Roberta?"

"Motherfucker figure." Ronnie grabbed another piece of bread and held his tongue out long enough for Audrey to see his tonsils. "You see, Roberta pisses off too many people. Then she pissed me off. I was thinking of replacing her with Clarice," searching for more bread, lifting napkins, glasses. "But you've handled the place on weekends for Roberta when she took off with me. You're efficient. Come in on time. Keep to yourself. Don't have a big mouth. Mind your own business. Don't gossip. In fact, you're the quietest woman I ever met." He reached over to the next table and stole the bread basket. "I heard you were once married to a thief."

"You *heard*?"

Staring at her blue eyes and light brown hair. A rainy-day girl who sits by the window. "People talk."

"Who in particular?"

Ronnie said, "You know her husband?"

"*Whose* husband?"

"Roberta's. The murderer."

"Murderer?"

"Yeah, one getting out of prison."

"If you mean Roy LaHood, he's not a murderer."

Ronnie sat back, arms folded. "What you mean is that he got away with it on a technicality. Roberta told me all about it."

"The guy Roy shot was stealing from them. He was also abusing her. Why're you so interested in Roy, anyway?"

"We're having dinner. Talking. You wanna talk football?"

"No, I wanna know why you're so interested in Roy. And don't tell me we're just talking."

"He murdered someone."

"You were there, Ronnie?"

"No."

"So how do you know?"

"There was a corpse."

"I'm talking about intention."

"He killed someone, period."

"The problem using the word 'kill,'" Audrey said, "is that you make Roy out to be someone he isn't."

"Which is what?"

"A murderer."

Ronnie almost laughed. "Somebody died because of him."

"Get to the point."

"I'd say you got a thing for this guy."

"You sound like you're worried."

"*Worried?*"

"Yeah, that he might do something to you."

"He killed Roberta's last lover. It's only rational to assume that he'll do it again."

"Get a gun if you're scared."

Ronnie, patting his waistband. "I got one and know how to use it."

"I heard you didn't like guns."

"I don't."

"Something about your brother, Frankie. Back in Jersey. Something went wrong."

Ronnie, not interested in talking about the past, reached for another piece of bread. "You know about the peephole?"

Audrey had no idea what he meant.

"One in the Executive Room. Where you dance with the clients."

"You put a *peephole* in there?"

Ronnie shrugged. "You could say I've made a study of you over the time you've been with us. You get the clients to think they can do anything they want with you. Then you push them away and make them come back for more. Like Julia on the pole. A beautiful tease, but a woman your age with your looks could easily find a man with more than enough money to buy you anything you wanted. So why waste your time being a tease?"

"Who says I'm wasting my time?"

"I do. Take advantage of what you have. Find someone who appreciates *what* you have."

"Like *you*?"

"Audrey," Ronnie leaning in, trying to touch her hand, "listen to me. You could have anything you want in this world. I see women up and down Palm Beach with half your looks, half your age, never once opening the door to their car." He set his glass down. "What I'm saying is be smart for once in your life."

"You think I wanna be the next Roberta?"

Ronnie said, "No. I'm looking for a woman with substance this time."

"You mean Clarice?"
"She's smarter than you think."
"Okay. What kind of offer are you making?"
"Something genuine."
"Like what?"
"Everything's negotiable."
"I'm not."
"I can give you what you want."
"What do I want, Ronnie?"
"You tell me."
"I need someone to talk to."
"You'll talk to me."
"I can't talk to you."
"You're talking to me now."
"Yeah, like I was talking to the gas-station attendant before."

"He can't pay the two hundred fifty thousand for Julia's college education. But I can. I've got influence, connections. I can get Julia into Duke. Help her move up in this world," pointing at the Blue Devil coming with their plates. "The middle class is dead, Audrey. Finished. Seven people at Apple, Facebook, Google can do the job of one hundred. We hire apps not people. The world has changed. Get on board. Don't be left behind is all I'm saying."

Audrey looked at the Blue Devil—so clean-cut she bled. "I thought you wanted me to manage a club you're opening somewhere out of state."

"I'm closing the Executive Room. You're going to be out of a job."

"Why are you closing it?"

"Roberta says it gives the club the wrong reputation. And besides that, I got an app coming out called Uber-Girls. You know what Uber is?"

"What about it?"

"I'm moving my business online, where off-line content and online services are combined. You download the app and you've downloaded my club. Reserve the girl of your choice for a lap dance, whatever, all guaranteed. The industry's changing, and I'm leading the charge. So let's be honest."

"About what?"

"Ten years you're fifty. Twenty years: sixty. The lines in your face will deepen. The folds under your eyes, widen. The skin on you neck and arms, sag. The onset of old age will be no less shocking than the onset of puberty, but less rewarding. That's where I come in. Money and good living can change all that," lifting up his glass like it was a done deal. "Why don't we take a ride on my yacht tonight? Up and down the coast. Show you the neighborhood. Your *new* neighborhood."

Audrey pushed her plate away. "No thanks."

"Stop fighting yourself."

"I get seasick."

"Not on my boat."

"You're not my type, Ronnie."

"How would you know?"

"The same way I know a stove is hot."

"You haven't even touched me."

"I've gotten close enough."

Ronnie sat back like he'd been burned. "Okay—You're honest. I like that. You're the kind of person I could use in the business end of the organization. You'll always give it to me straight. I'd like you to consider my generous offer. There's no rush. Take it step by step, but you gotta take that first step."

"I'm already in your organization."

"But you're not part of the team."

"Whose team?"

"My special team."

Audrey got up. "Ronnie, the only person on your special team is you." She left a twenty on the table and headed home.

CHAPTER ELEVEN

Audrey angled the monster through the dirt path that led to her bungalow and cut the throbbing Italian motor. Gertie Eccles was already out the doorway. "There's somebody been at your place, Audrey," pointing to a cigarette that glowed from the beach. "I hope it ain't that gang been robbing the pensioners up and down the highway."

"Gertie, *put* that gun away."

"Police says it's some biker bunch. Leaves old folks nothing as if they had anything to begin with."

"If you're so worried, stay inside and lock your door."

"I'll tell ya what worries me, Audrey. I been up all night with Herb 'cause of that arrhythmia of his."

"I thought he was on a medication."

"I thought so too, Audrey, but I had to run down the road to get Lena, that hospital nurse, when I saw the snooper near your bungalow a second time. I thought it was maybe Herb's nephew, Bobby, come all the way up from New York City to harm me. You know how he hates me for no good reason. A person got a right to protect herself."

Audrey was at her front door, key in hand.

Gertie said, "Maybe there's something you'd like to tell me," pointing her thirty-eight Shorty at the beach.

"There's nothing to tell you."

"Well, I'll stay here. Keep an eye out. Just in case."

"As long as you don't fire that gun, I don't care what you do."

Audrey opened the door to her bungalow and went to the big window that faced the ocean. The beach was still. Everything seemed normal. Nothing inside had been touched, including the silence that followed her wherever she went. She sat on the living room couch, Indian style, and waited. Sometime later she woke up to a striking match. A man's face appeared in the geometry of the glow. It was fragmented, distant, brittle in the flame. Ten years long and empty.

Audrey calmly but sternly said, "How dare you break into my home?"

"I love you."

"Get out."

CHAPTER TWELVE

Bobby Braren, Herb's nephew in New York City, looked up at the basement pipes that were dripping on his head. He wiped away the water then put his mobile phone back to his ear. "Gertie, what do you mean my uncle Herb's dying?" Another drip. The contractors were supposed to have fixed the pipes, redone the air-conditioning system, made the office building more environmentally friendly, but that was before Wall Street collapsed in September of 2008 and the country's money suddenly disappeared. The magician who had been waving the magic wand had suddenly waved himself away. So Bobby sold half his building to a sleazy financial group that knew something about getting retirees to convert their US government guaranteed fixed pensions for more riskier non-guaranteed assets all for a fat fee and the opportunity to lose every cent they had. Bobby had his own concerns. "Are *you* saying my uncle's dying, or did the *doctors* tell you he's dying?"

Gertie, squeezing the phone to her ear. "Look, Bobby. My age, ya know when someone's on the way. I don't need a person with a stethoscope to point where the graveyard is."

"He had another heart attack?"

"*You* don't listen, Bobby."

"I've been listening to you for ten minutes."

"Then your ears are stuffed. Last time y'all wasn't speaking. Now, bless his heart, he points at your photo all day long and says, till he's blue in the face, how you're the last of the line. Says all he's got is you, like *you* was anything special."

"Did my uncle say he's dying?"

"He just asks for ya, Bobby."

"Gertie, you're absolutely sure he's really dying?"

"Wanna wait till he's dead?"

"I'm just asking."

"What I should do, Bobby, is to put on the phone this colored boy who's a friend of my neighbor, Audrey. Remember her? That real pretty gal ya got all excited over last time ya was here? I caught the boy on his way out of her bungalow and invited him over."

"What's he gotta do with me?"

"I'll tell ya what he's gotta do with you. He was the most successful cat burglar in the history of the transgression. Never once was him and his partner caught until one of 'em got involved with a billionariess woman they robbed. That's the thing that'll make this talking picture such a big hit and us a fortune."

"*What* talking picture?"

"One you're gonna make with me. One I'm working on with Roy LaHood. That's his name, the cat burglar, one who wrote it all down in a correctional facility. I been looking it over just now. He left it at my neighbor's this morning after trying to make love to her. I took it 'cause she wasn't into it, and boy did I land on a gold mine. It's got the plot and the arc what you're always talking about and all the dough piling up. I'm warning ya, Bobby: better sit down and work out a deal with me before I do it with someone else."

"You're a movie producer now?"

"Bobby, you been living in that damn lying city for so long that when ya do stumble upon the truth, it's already been starved dead. Your problem is you and your world-famous artist girlfriend, Wanda, is always talking up some story to address the world's problems because y'all wanna be taken so seriously. What y'all don't understand is that people want to avoid the world's problems. By the way, Roy plays golf under seventy as if anything over is a disease to run away from." Jabbing her finger at the manuscript. "And this colored boy knows how to write."

"Gertie. Do me a favor. Just this once. Stop calling African Americans 'colored.'"

"Want me to call 'em 'white'?"

Bobby stepped away from another drip. "You've seen him play golf, or is he just lying?"

"*Lying?*" Turning to the opening page and pointing with her finger. "Roy LaHood's part Ibitoupa Indian. Knows the Yazoo better than a blue sucker and—wait a second, Bobby." Looking over her shoulder. "Your uncle's stuck in his Big Boy again and can't get out." She let the phone hang on its cord.

CHAPTER THIRTEEN

West Palm Beach International Airport. Bobby Braren drove out of Alamo with a Chevy economy instead of the Caddy. His previous visit, Gertie took the Caddy for a spin, lost a rim, couldn't figure out how to turn off the wipers, and then crashed into a bicycle. The Caddy looked like a stock car after the first trip around the block.

Bobby reached for his phone and called his uncle to let him know he was minutes away, but there was no answer. He tried again. Still no answer. Maybe he was too late. Bobby began wiping away the tears. Thinking of tough old Uncle Herb. The last of his Borscht Belt relatives. The man who grew up in a world of felt hats and slow cooking. Cigarettes in the morning. Cigars in the evening. And he sweated the old-fashioned way: through everything and with a fresser's grin. He had wurst-thick hands that had a plumber's knack for getting at things. A man of the old world with no formal education. Just street smarts and a jaywalker's spring to his step. But it was his big warm smile and the way he'd rub the top of Bobby's head and say, *Gimme some luck, kid* that made Bobby glad to be one of the tribe. He pulled up in front of his uncle's bungalow, hoping that the worst hadn't yet happened. Gertie leaped into the passenger side of the Chevy like she was going to carjack him.

"Bobby, when ya wake up, maybe ya can tell me why ya rented this piece of junk instead of a Caddy."

"Who's the girl?" His eye on Julia, walking out of her bungalow. Heading toward the beach. Surfboard in tow. Bikini as wide as a match cover.

"Julia, one I been trying to tell ya about on the phone. Her pretty mama's the one ya eyeballed last time. See, Julia's gonna be casted in our talking picture, but I gotta warn ya, Bobby: she's no one's fool."

Maybe, but Bobby was wondering how long it would take to escape Gertie, change into his Speedo—his uncle would have to live a little longer.

"She does what she wants, this girl, but then the way she looks, Bobby, you'll do what she wants," watching her paddle out to a wave.

Julia duck dived out beyond the breakers, unaware of the landlubbers, as she scanned the glazed horizon. When the right wave came along, she turned to shore and rode it in until there was nothing left of the bull.

Gertie yanked Bobby. "We better go inside, see how your uncle's doing."

Julia noticed the stranger in the distant. He had that familiar trance. The fixed gaze of a man overdue for something good. Gertie had already told her about Bobby. Julia didn't care. "I'm not interested in old men."

"Bobby ain't old, Julia. *Herb's* the one who's old."

"I don't care. Keep him away from me."

"Bobby can make you a movie star."

"I don't want to be a movie star."

"Well, yer wasting your time wanting to be a doctor. All they do is get sued."

"You're the one wasting your time, and if you bring him near me, you're in big trouble."

"Why do ya always have to get nasty when folks try and help ya, Julia?"

"Because they're helping *themselves*."

Gertie, nudging Bobby, "I think Julia's spotted us."

The person she spotted was Roy LaHood standing in the doorway of Herb's bungalow. Gertie had notified him that Bobby would be arriving. Told him to hurry up over and close the deal.

Bobby, now inside the bungalow, stared at the breathing apparatus attached to the double canisters on the floor by the side of Herb's Big Boy. The little bungalow was more than just dirty. Dust balls gathered like moss around a tree. The cannula hose that snaked up Uncle Herb's chest looked more alive than he did as it forked into his nose. His hands were lousy and frail, with nails the shade of slate. He had gotten thinner, hollower. His skin, just links of wrinkles. The one-time scrapper from 50 Eldridge Street, block south of Hester, looked more like a piece of scrap in his rumpled, soiled clothesline pajamas. His eyes, distant and wet, were aimless and numb. It took more than a moment for the old man to recognize his nephew, but when he did, the smile broke through like sunshine, and all the bad feelings vanished. Bobby put his hand on his uncle's tender shoulder.

"How're you feeling, Uncle Herb?"

Herb reached out his thin head at what he couldn't see. "Oiy! Ich bin farblundzhen!"

Gertie said, "He's telling ya he wants you to sit down, Bobby."

"That's *not* what he said."

"Don't you tell me what he said," as she wiped the old man's forehead to show she was attentive. "Roy, this here is Bobby Braren, the talking picture producer. He's a Yankee and got bad manners but knows how to make money."

Bobby leaned into his uncle and whispered, so only he could hear, "Uncle Herb, tell me if this woman's been taking care of you."

Uncle Herb tried to move his head, but the weakness in his neck and the stiffness of tubes attached to his nose made him cry, "Zis ah narish froy!"

Gertie said, "He says to sit down, Bobby. You'll get him excited if ya don't."

"That's *not* what he said."

"*Yeah?* Well, I'm the one taking care of your uncle while you're far away in New York City. You farshtunkiner good-for-nothing," moving in between Bobby and Herb, taking the old man's hand in hers like it was her own.

Roy, just a few feet away, wasn't sure what to make of Bobby with his curly brown tangled hair. His shoulders stooped like a man in the middle of Manhattan crosstown traffic whose thoughts were stored in other places besides his head. Bobby had his eye on Roy, as well. He was big. Country. A two-legged homily that amplified small-town comfort with a smile that would have to be rationed or dismissed in a big overcrowded city where anyone with a grin was guilty of being more than just sociable. Roy extended his hand, Rotary Club style. Bobby stared at the big paw. He turned back to Gertie, disgusted at all the junk she had stuffed into the small bungalow since having first arrived, already well into her eighties: something the undertaker had taken notice of when going on his rounds.

Roy, feeling the coolness, tried to break the ice. "I hear you're from New York City, Bobby."

"Uh yeah."

"Manhattan?"

"Uh yeah."

"Upper West Side?"

"Uh no."

"Where?

"Tribeca."

Roy said, "My wife had a few gigs singing in clubs downtown. We lived over on Bleecker by the IND Line. Block down from Monte's over on MacDougal. Never had to lift a griddle in twelve months. You ever hear of the Café Wha?"

Bobby turned to the intruder.

Roy said, "Thelma, here, tells me you're in the real-estate business. You one of them brokers come Sunday morning with the bagels?"

"No."

"You do know what a bagel is?"

Bobby stared at the tall man. "Yeah, I know what a bagel is. You know what a pain in the ass is?"

Bobby turned back to his uncle propped up on double pillows. Glasses short of his ears. Old slippers with a toe poking through. Bobby was nauseated from the sickly smell that pervaded the bungalow. It had been there when he'd walked in, but now it was heavier, deeper, like molten sludge. He stared at his uncle, once the strapping oysvorf who overcame adversity and bigotry with methods others more fortunate could avoid. He hadn't been washed for days. His hair, thick with sweat and oil. His teeth, stained and coated with plaque. Bobby got another tap on the shoulder. "Your aunt Thelma, here, tells me you produce movies."

"She's *not* my aunt, and her name's *Gertie*."

Bobby watched Gertie fake it as she took Herb's pulse. He couldn't stand the woman.

Gertie said, "His arrhythmia's back. He's breathing hard. I don't know to give him more amiodarone or not, Bobby. I called the doctor's service line before. They said to bring him in the morning for an EKG, but they can't cardiovert 'cause of his frailty or something."

Roy said to Bobby, "What kinda flicks you and Wanda into?"

Bobby said to Gertie, "What's amiodarone?"

"It's what they give to keep the heart steady."

"I know, but *what* the hell is it?"

"Ya think I'm a doctor?"

Bobby said, "Uncle Herb. You wanna go back to the hospital?"

Gertie said, "I just got him out."

Bobby said, "*Maybe* he needs to go back."

Roy said, "I hear that new flick of yours and Wanda's been green-lighted."

Bobby said to Roy, "Do fucking you mind?" Trying to hold his stare at the man twice his size.

Gertie said, "Y'all wanna go to the emergency room, we can go, Bobby."

"I think we better."

"Well, then let's go, but the drugs is supposed to take some time before the heart finally gets back into sinus. That's what the doctors call it. It could take another few days or weeks, they said. They're not sure. I took your uncle down the other day thinking it was real bad like now, and the doctor she says to give it more time. But I don't know, Bobby. I just don't know. I'm not as confident as they all are."

Bobby said, "Why didn't you keep him there?"

"Where?"

"The hospital."

"Well, the hospital is always getting in new patients and they said your uncle would be more comfortable at home."

"Was my uncle complaining he wanted to go home?"

"Tell ya the truth, Bobby, I ain't too sure he didn't think he already was at home. Look, I know how ya feel, but I been going at it like this for a while, and I suppose somebody walks in from nowhere could think your uncle's worse than he really is. Now, if his condition ain't changed by morning, we'll just leave him in the hospital whether they like it or not."

Roy said to Bobby, "I hear your new flick's got Halle Berry playing a blind social worker who dies in a car crash right after she cuts her first album that turns into a megahit."

Turning to Roy, "Who the fuck told you that?"

"Wanda. Your girlfriend. One who wants to green-light my memoir. One who was on the phone with Thelma, here, before she and I got to talking. One who said she was sick of all the sentimental crap y'all make out in Hollywood."

Bobby stared at Gertie like he was going to knife her. "What's that vial in your hand?"

Gertie looked at the side table with about thirty prescription bottles. "Which vial?"

"The goddamn one in your hand."

"Ya don't have to talk to me like that, Bobby."

"*Give* it to me."

Gertie handed it over. "Look, Bobby, I'm doing everything I can for your uncle while you're far away in New York and California, getting rich making talking pictures and selling real estate and fancy-schmancy art. Ya wanna take care of your uncle? Go ahead. There ain't no one stopping ya. But don't yell at me for doing all your work."

Bobby studied the vial as if concentration alone might cause a breakthrough in his uncle's ailment.

Roy said, "Wanda's now in the air."

Bobby looked up. "*What* air?"

"Flying."

"Where?"

"Here.

Gertie added, "Should be landing any minute."

Bobby went after Gertie.

Roy stepped in. "I got her flight number and arrival gate. You wanna pick Wanda up, Bobby, or you want me to?"

Herb made a sick sucking noise. Then he opened his eyes as if a camera had flashed. He shot out a wad of phlegm.

Gertie hollered, "Bobby, run to the kitchen. There's a plastic bottle with a long straw by the sink. Fill it up with water and bring the Wipees. *Hurry up,* Bobby. He's all messy at the mouth."

Bobby returned with the plastic bottle and the box of Wipees, but someone wasn't there.

Gertie said, "Roy's gone to the airport."

CHAPTER FOURTEEN

Roberta gripped onto her phone as if it were Roy's throat. "Your life's going to be *very* short if you so much as go near Ronnie's safes."

"Tell you what, Roberta. You be nice and the Tooth Fairy will put something under your pillow." He dropped the call.

Roberta texted him: *Ronnie's new girlfriend Clarice wants to know if ur going to kill him. What should I tell her?*

Roy texted back: *GFY*

Wanda was in a crowd of dazed passengers emerging on the curb with its luggage and pale skin. She dazzled them with Bedouin earrings that touched her shoulders. Gypsy rings, alchemic and cloudy, that changed color with her moods. She grabbed her camera and documented the scene even though she was its central player kitted in skin-tight blue jeans, black city high heeled boots with quirky starps, chunky soles, and dampened with layers of guardsman polish. She was regimental ready and ready for action: one of those horny women who couldn't hide it. A touch was all she needed and not for a lack of regular sex, but an eagerness and an ability to hug for long periods of time and freely sweat that had her always on alert. She caught sight of Roy, Crystal, the truck, and moved toward them at a runway gallop.

Roy tossed Wanda's carry-on in the Raptor's flatbed and held the passenger door open as she took more photos. Roy thinking that's what these downtown artsy people do as they accumulate moments onto contact sheets, and then to prints, canvasses, installations, and then off to galleries before moving on to auction houses, museums, and the next interview.

Wanda, flattered by the Southern hospitality, was surprised Roy was dark. It had been obvious from his ripe diction that he was from the Deep South, which caused her to freely indulge in Yankee liable, such as whiskered colonels, gun-totin' buckras, cornbread mammies, and the slowness of warm-weather walking and church-scrubbed whiteness. But a field hand with dust on his chin wasn't what she was expecting. She eagerly hopped into the truck and panted like a big cat.

She took to Roy, immediately and fraternally. He had the energy of the hunter. The prowler's slow-moving bristle. The stride of the cheetah hotfoot in the savannah. She could see he wasn't a man who wanted to save the world or strike it down with his art. His concerns were of the now. How to get it. Keep it. And though their thighs were barely touching, at moments rubbing, it was as if Roy was already inside her as she closed her lips against a thoughtless moan that filled the quiet cabin. She turned back to the mounted gun rack to officiate the moment, but to her surprise there was only a parking sticker.

Roy whistled. "Finished reading my manuscript?"

"Right in the middle of it."

"Whaddya think so far?"

She looked into his big whirling eyes. "So far so good."

CHAPTER FIFTEEN

Ronnie Harrison was standing before a full-length mirror in his big walk-in closet: the size of any Manhattan one-bedroom apartment. He was thinking: dressy or short-sleeves casual? Turnbull & Asser or Sean John? Buttons open to the sternum or polo collar flipped up Argentinean?

Ronnie went with the blue striped Turnbull. He placed the rest of his outfit: his Pireneo black crocs and Hugo Boss jeans on his bed and made a flat man. An orange Ralph Lauren polo shirt with the oversized gelding on the breast that screamed *I'm A Polo Player You're Not* was backup. Clarice, dressed and starved, opened the bedroom door and handed Ronnie a pile of printouts. She looked at the flat man on the bed then at Ronnie.

"Ronnie, you was supposed to be dressed an hour ago."

He took the printouts Clarice had just downloaded from the Internet and pointed to the photo of Raydel Palmero. "This the guy Roy LaHood stood his ground?"

"Yeah, and if I don't eat supper soon, I won't stand my ground."

The big white leather surround chair let out a big breath as Ronnie slumped into it. He stared at the photo of Raydel Palmero in jockey shorts and socks, shoes flipped over, face in a pool of blood that ran from his mouth to the edge of Roberta's bed. His open eyes retained the shock they received the moment the forty caliber entered his skull. Ronnie turned the page to the mug shot of Roy LaHood.

Clarice said, "You want me to cancel the reservations at Alfredo's? Everybody says Sultan Boca is the place to go."

Studying the height grid behind Roy, Ronnie said, "He's that tall?"

Clarice looked at the photo. "Six feet six, in the NBA, is short."

"LaHood was in the NBA?"

"I'm just making a point."

"Don't."

Ronnie read through the rest of the printouts: the first trial and then the retrial that got the conviction overturned. The prosecutor said, *"This is a miscarriage of justice and a signal to anyone wishing to commit murder that you can get away with crime by simply manipulating the evidence."*

Roy's defense lawyer, Jenny Sullivan, who could make you feel you were under a tree when lightning strikes, rebutted with, *"What the state is saying is that a person's innocence shouldn't get in the way of the prosecutor's conviction record."*

Ronnie skipped over to another article, dated 1998. A Palm Beach County Robbery Squad lieutenant said, *"We believe LaHood and Gibbs to be the prime suspects of a series of jewel heists along the Gold Coast over the past several years. They have been difficult to apprehend because they operate counterintuitively to the criminal and law enforcement MO."*

One of the reporters asked the lieutenant what he had meant by "counterintuitively." The cop said, "They walk in and out of a location during suppertime like they're part of the family. Except they don't sit down and eat."

Ronnie flipped back to the photo of Raydel Palmero on Roberta's blood-stained ivory Berber carpet.

Clarice, hands on her hips, chin down like a bull. "Ronnie, if we eat at midnight again, I'm leaving you."

Ronnie had a better idea. He grabbed a pretzel, put the printouts on the side dresser, and said to Clarice, "Make me another drink."

Clarice did an about-face and stormed out of the bedroom.

Ronnie chewed into his phone as he dialed his lawyer. "Buford? Ronnie. Think you could stop by the house tomorrow?"

Buford Harlen said, "Tomorrow? I think I'm busy. In fact—I'm busy all week long. Why don't you come on down to the office?"

"I can't. I got some of the girls from the club coming over for a splash in the pool."

"You mean *after* work?"

"After work. Before work. Whenever you want."

"I don't know, Ronnie. I'm supposed to bill you for those hours."

"Bring your swimsuit, Buford. The girls will be in the pool."

"The blond one? Will she be there?"

"Which blond one?"

"Julia."

"Yeah, sure. They'll all be here."

"You're lying to me."

"Buford, there's a lot of girls in this world. Why do you want her?"

"I more than want her, Ronnie."

"You're wasting your time."

"I'll be the judge of that."

"Buford, she's not like some of the other girls at the club you've had fun with."

"You misunderstand my intentions."

"I misunderstand nothing. I'll see you noon, tomorrow. Bring all the information you can get on a Roy LaHood. He just got released from Starke. I want you to figure out a way to send him back."

"Ronnie, you said come over for a swim, not a conference."

"We gotta talk about something."

"I'll have to bill you then."

"You want girls there?"

"Just make sure Julia's there."

"Buford, I already told her you're coming. She can't wait. But if you want a conference, we'll meet in your office. I leave it up to you."

Buford, eager. "What did she say?"

"Who?"

"*Julia.*"

"Come over tomorrow and find out."

Ronnie hung up and called Julia. It took five rings.

"I'm busy, Ronnie."

"Duke is the school to go."

"You got the cash to pay for it?"

"I got whatever you want, Julia."

"That school costs sixty-thousand bricks a semester and it's going up next year."

"Julia, how many times I have to tell you? You meet the right people in the right schools, and I know someone who can more than get you in."

"All you know are creeps, Ronnie."

"All right. Go to some community college. Some small-town nothing college. But it's not the place to get ahead."

"It is for my budget."

"We can fix that. You know that lawyer who likes you?"

She reminded Ronnie, "There are a lot of lawyers who like me Wednesday through Saturday."

"I mean *my* lawyer. I introduced him to you at the club a dozen times. Buford Harlen. Not bad looking, either. He's got more influence than anyone I know, and the kid is smart."

"He's an old man."

"You think thirty-eight is old?"

"I think twenty-five is old."

"Julia, the guy went to Duke. His family donates truckloads of cash."

"You want me to run around topless."

"Whoever said that? I just want you to get ahead in life. Not like your mother. No ambition. Nothing."

"Lay off my mother."

"Julia, one day you're gonna be an old lady. This boy Buford is worth a ton of money. Knows a lot of people with influence. All you have to do is be nice, and you'll get everything you want in life."

"Ronnie, how do you be nice to a guy without fucking him?"

"Julia, I fired your mother. I can fire you."

"Go ahead, Ronnie, but Roberta already told me you invite Buford over the house to see the girls topless in the pool, so you don't have to go to his office and pay the seven-hundred-dollar-an-hour billing fee. You want me to run around topless? The price is four hundred dollars an hour. It's a bargain."

"Roberta's a real piece of shit."

"You wanna pay the seven hundred?"

"How about three fifty?"

"Geezuz, Ronnie."

CHAPTER SIXTEEN

The following day Ronnie Harrison was sprawled out on a big white lounge chair by the vanishing-edge pool just yards from the beachfront. Alongside him was an eager second-string lover who looked like he hadn't played all season.

Ronnie said to Buford, "Don't worry. She's here."

Buford worried. Ronnie didn't tell him Julia was late. Some surfing lesson. Some lab work. Some college interview she had to get ready for the following day.

Buford, in suit and tie, briefcase in hand, "Where are the other girls?"

A motorcycle tore through the driveway gravel.

Buford turned to Ronnie, "Is that Julia?"

It was, but she had her own plans and went upstairs to wind down in the master bedroom Jacuzzi.

Ronnie said, "Get in your trunks, Buford. Relax. I got lunch coming. Best BLTs you ever had." He raised a tall glass of beer as a toast.

Buford was having none of it. "You said there'd be girls in the pool. The goddamn pool is empty. Unless you've got invisible girls."

Ronnie handed him a cold beer and opened his arms like he was welcoming home an old friend. "Buford. Enjoy yourself. Life's good. Julia's getting ready just for you. Clarice will be down any second."

"*Clarice?*"

"Yeah, the girl you once dated."

"I don't wanna see her," but he did.

She was up against the floor-to-ceiling bedroom window holding her nose with a hand towel; the housemaid, arms around her shoulders to give her comfort.

Ronnie got up from his chair. "Excuse me."

He met Clarice and the maid at the bottom of the grand stairway. Clarice was wearing a white two-piece streaked with blood. "Fire that bitch, or I'm leaving you and the fucking club."

"You mind telling me what happened?"

"Julia's *paying* for my new nose."

A moment later Clarice was in the housemaid's Kia as it reversed and plowed through the driveway to the emergency room.

Clarice had been doing her makeup when Julia walked into the bedroom and headed straight for the Jacuzzi. Clarice said, "Get the fuck out of my bathroom."

Julia laughed, "Jacuzzis are the worst thing for fake tits."

Clarice took a swing at Julia, but Julia had already mastered the technique of disarming and disabling a pain in the neck.

Ronnie, now at the top of the stairway, could hear the Jacuzzi pump going. He walked into the bathroom and found Julia chin deep in foaming water. She was feeling nothing. Thinking nothing. Not even there. Ronnie cut off the Jacuzzi. The water turned glass still. "The hell happened to you and Clarice?"

"Turn the goddamn Jacuzzi back on, Ronnie."

"You could've killed her."

"You're so worried? How come you're not with her?"

"You think I'm a doctor?"

Julia, stepping out of the water. "Why are men such self-absorbed pieces of shit?"

"This is not the first time you hit somebody. That guy in Boca is suing the club for driving his Mercedes off the dock."

"Ronnie, give me the money for this stunt, or I'm leaving."

Julia cruised down the big wide stairway. Ronnie peeled off four one-hundred-dollar bills. Julia took the money and sailed through the living room, out the big sliding doors to the pool patio, past the Duke-trained lawyer sweating in the lounge chair, and hollered, "*Hey*, Buford," before diving into the pool.

Ronnie, coming from behind, put a hand on Buford's shoulder. "I don't think she's the girl for you."

Buford watched Julia turn laps like pages. "She's supposed to be topless."

Ronnie guided Buford back to his chair. "Give her a minute. What'd you find out about Roy LaHood?"

But the leash to Buford's heart had already snapped. His eyes drifted into the blinding Florida sun like a man measuring it against an oasis far out into the horizon, calculating if he could get there before he died of thirst. Buford breathed in the salty ocean air as if it were the young woman's sweat.

Ronnie took the files from the lawyer's briefcase and went through them. "I can't make out all this legal mumbo jumbo."

Buford didn't care. His eyes were weightless orbs pinned to a cloud.

"Buford—Are you *there?*"

He watched Julia flip over at the far end of the pool. Swim another lap. Then dive off the board as his heart leaped.

"Buford, *wake* up. What's this 'Four-Minute Burglar' stuff I'm reading?" Ronnie slapped Buford hard on the arm.

He swung around like a door opened by a swift gust of wind.

"I said, what's this 'Four-Minute Burglar' stuff I'm reading?"

"That's how long it took."

"How long *what* took?"

"For LaHood and Gibbs to get in and out of a location," pointing to the other document.

Julia did a jackknife then drilled the length of the pool. Buford thought the girl swam better than a fish. "You're in my way, Ronnie."

"How dangerous is this LaHood?"

Buford, straining to see the pool, "I don't know."

Ronnie took him by the shoulders. "You think this LaHood will try and shoot me because I was with his wife?"

"You should have thought of that before you went out with Roberta."

Ronnie said, "At the time LaHood was looking at a twenty-five-year bid."

"Now he isn't."

"You think he'll try and kill me?"

"Ask Roberta."

"I did."

"What did she say?"

"She had a big grin on her face." There was none on Ronnie's.

Buford, eyes on Julia plowing through the water. "You were smart to get rid of Roberta."

"I'm beginning to think it would have been better had I kept her."

Julia submerged and returned to the underworld where beauties rested and replenished.

"Roberta's now out of your life, Ronnie. There's no immediate cause for LaHood to come after you other than—" Getting a glimpse of Julia surfacing at the other end of the pool.

"What?"

"Residual cause."

"What's that?"

"See it as a latent risk, not as an imminent threat, Ronnie."
"I don't understand."
"He's not a killer."
Julia, swimming on her back.
"What do you mean he's not a killer? Roy LaHood killed Raydel Palmero."
Julia, swimming prone.
Buford said, "It was Roberta's gun that was discharged at the scene."
"So?"
"LaHood's lawyer showed that the shooting was not premeditated. It was a home invasion, and LaHood had stood his ground. Something the first lawyer should've made clear."
"Everyone knows that's bullshit. LaHood killed Palmero."
"Ronnie, if the courts relied on public opinion—and I don't mean the Supreme Court's opinion, necessarily, because you can make an argument those judges are as fucked up as everyone else—this world would really be a mess; and, anyway, in all their years, LaHood and Gibbs never once used a gun on a job."
"You're telling me LaHood and Gibbs robbed without a gun?"
"That's the way they operated and the jury loved it."
"What if an angry homeowner was armed?"
Julia threw her arms up on the pool ledge.
"I'm not a thief, Ronnie. Just a lawyer."
"What thief doesn't carry a gun?"
Julia lifted herself onto the ledge and grabbed a towel.
"Buford, I *asked* you a question."
He turned to Ronnie. "The woman who put Gibbs away said he didn't even have so much as a toothpick on him."
"Maybe he had the keys to the house?"
"No. He came in with a smile and a handshake like the Fuller Brush Man; then they fell in love. You ever hear of Leyland Johnson?"

Ronnie said, "You mean that billionaire banker over in Palm Beach?"

"Yeah."

"Gibbs had an affair with his wife?"

Buford glanced at his watch. Almost one o'clock. Julia, still not topless.

"*Answer* me, Buford?"

"Mrs. Johnson was home alone on a Monday night."

"Who *isn't?*"

"I don't know, but her husband was away on a business trip. She's so disoriented from all the venlafaxine, she's thinking Leyland's downstairs watching TV. Gibbs walks into the master bedroom. Introduces himself. Takes the pills out of her hand. Soon they're at it."

Ronnie said, "He's that good-looking?"

Buford turned back to Julia. "It's one o'clock, Ronnie."

"Answer my question."

"She's still not topless.

"Is he *that* good-looking?"

"I don't know. I never met him, but everybody likes Gibbs. Even the judge who sent him away gave him a hug."

"You said something on the phone about LaHood and Gibbs being in the army."

Julia, taking off her top.

"Rangers. Iraq."

"When?"

"First Bush."

Julia, turning her back to them.

"Buford, they see action?"

"Unless their eyes were closed."

"You think that nigger'll kill me for fucking his wife?"

"Call him 'nigger,' he will," trying to get a better look at Julia.

"If you think I am afraid of LaHood, I'm not."

"You're a very tough guy, Ronnie. A real shtarker, as my Hebrew friends say," trying to free himself of Ronnie's grip.

"I bought a gun, Buford."

"I thought you hated guns."

"I hate dying, too."

"You forget your brother got a bullet in the head back in Jersey."

"Buford, what am I supposed to do somebody comes after me? Always think of my brother?"

"Think of yourself."

Ronnie grabbed Buford by the arm as if he were about to slip. "Buford—Have you ever killed somebody?"

Staring at Ronnie, "That's irrelevant to this whole conversation."

"Why is it irrelevant?"

"Because what's at point isn't if *I* killed someone. It's whether you have, Ronnie. Whether you'll be in a normal state of mind when the moment comes *and* if such a notion is possible when you're under stress. Something they forgot to take into consideration when they passed Stand Your Ground, because no one is in a rational state of mind, let alone reasonable when under stress. Just scared shitless or nuts."

"What do you mean by '*normal* state of mind'?"

Julia, prone. Buford, crouching. "When you bought that gun, were you in a normal state of mind?"

The salesman in the gun shop hadn't asked Ronnie that question when he walked in. He just took Ronnie out back. Let him fire a few rounds at the bad-guy target with the blacked-out figure in the lunge position at twenty-five feet to get the feel of what it would be like to down a jealous husband—of course, *only* if Ronnie should be in a situation where it would be legally permissible, such as Stand Your Ground: a law that removed any requirement of retreat. The salesman told Ronnie he then could basically do what the fuck he wanted.

Ronnie said to the salesman, "Look, my brother, Frankie, knew all about guns. One night he throws a gumba out of a club in Jersey. The grease ball comes back with a gun. My brother was ready."

The salesman said, "Good."

"It jammed."

"What?"

"My brother's gun."

The salesman shrugged.

"I need a gun that won't jam."

The salesman said, "Don't worry," and brought Ronnie a cup of coffee from the reloader's bench and assured him that the statistical average of guns jamming was very low and that Frankie's accident was way off the bell curve and that all gun exchanges occur within a distance of eight feet or less and in full view. "You'll see the bad guy like you're seeing me. You'll kill the motherfucker just as he reaches for it."

Ronnie looked up from the burned coffee in the white Styrofoam cup and said to the gun salesman, "You sell bulletproof vests?"

"Sure, Mr. Harrison, whatever you want, we got. Except courage. That we can't sell you."

Ronnie went after Buford, who was already halfway down the pool. "Buford, when you said, 'Was I in a normal state of mind?' Did you mean courage?"

"Ronnie, if you have to ask that question, I'd think twice about carrying a weapon."

Buford turned his attention back to Julia. He was going to bring her home. Introduce her to the folks. Tell them of his plans to marry her and how he'd never look at another woman until the bonds of life snapped. He fixed his tie. Smoothed his hair. Then proceeded to the edge of the pool and turned himself in. "Will you marry me?"

Julia looked up at her sweat-soaked suitor. "How much are you offering?"

"You don't understand."

"*What* don't I understand?"

"I love you."

"Write me a check for ten million dollars."

"I could do that."

"*Do* it."

"But I can't."

"Why?"

"How do you put a value on human life?"

Julia grabbed her towel. "The value was on your offer, not my life."

It was one o'clock. Julia left Buford there as she did the puddle of water at her feet. She had better things to do. Better men to dispose. Now it was Ronnie's turn to give advice. He put a comforting hand on Buford's lonely shoulder as they watched Julia peel away on her Monster 1200. "Buford, you want a beautiful woman? Buy her." And with an added pat, "Just don't let her know you're doing it," eating his own words.

CHAPTER SEVENTEEN

While Ronnie was admonishing Buford, Bobby Braren was tossing Gertie's dresses, shoes, picnic blouses, Sunday meetin' wigs, rubber girdles, Columbus washboard, galoshes, a Bible, a belt. Everything Gertie Eccles had owned was being dumped, dropped, shoved, tossed, and extruded from the tops of tables, corners, closets, sideboards, beds, inside shower curtains, and other places where you could push, shove and archive useless junk, including a handgun, which Bobby threw in the community garbage bin. Gertie went after it. Bobby dragged her away. "That's the last thing a fool like you needs."

Wanda said, "Bobby, I'm so sorry about your uncle Herb."

Her hard Detroit inflection, burnished by years of Canadian arctic winds and auto plants, caused her words to rust as soon as they were spoken.

Gertie, kneeling on the floor, tightened her grip on Wanda. "Honey, I got no place to go. No place to put my head. Not a dime to my name. What am I to do if all y'all leave me in the street and allow people like Bobby to abuse a poor old person with nothing but love in her heart?"

Wanda glared at Bobby.

Roy had his own ideas.

So did Bobby. He pushed Gertie out the bungalow, but she held onto the edge of the door, tooth and nail. It got to be a real tug-of-war until Gertie got the final shove and landed in the dirt path.

Roy said to Bobby, "You shouldn't've have hit her like that."

Bobby said, "You call this taking care of a person?" Pointing to his dead uncle, whose head barely completed a circle. His blue eyes, glassy, smoky, gray, flat. His mouth, an uneven gorge of phlegm and teeth. "The filth she kept my uncle in, just so she could have a rent-free place to stay."

Roy reminded Bobby, "You don't leave family to other folks."

"I don't know if I should be listening to you."

"In times like this, we all gotta pitch in."

"You mean like helping you make that movie of yours?"

"I'm trying to be decent, Bobby."

"Is that why you were sent to prison?"

Bobby leaned over his uncle, fought back the tears, and wondered how it all came to this. A bold fire of family that had crossed the Atlantic was now almost out. But not the memories nor the big old-fashioned faces of yesteryear that were a muddle of lumps and hard knocks. Pain and suffering etched into their skin. They were shteytl folks crated with home remedies. Low to the ground with stout appetites. Able to eat onions like apples. Fish, pickled or sliced. Geese, boiled or chilled. All with the backhand cut of a paring knife.

Roy, feeling Bobby's pain, quietly said, "Your uncle must've really meant something to you."

That only made Bobby feel worse. How could it be a question when it was so obviously a fact?

Roy added, "I'd be more'n glad to give you a hand," meaning the corpse.

"You want to give me a *hand?*" Looking down at his stiff dead uncle.

"Bobby, you'll have to notify the police. Make funeral arrangements. I can drive you over. Wait in the car. Be there for you."

"You don't even know me."

"Do I have to?" Using a softer tone, "*Bobby*—We got a dead man here."

"He's not a dead man. He's my uncle."

"In this heat you can't afford to let him stay overnight."

"If I want, he'll stay here for a fucking month."

"By morning they won't be able to fit him in a coffin."

"Why don't you go fuck yourself?"

"I'm just trying to be neighborly, Bobby."

"Get lost."

"If that's what you want."

"*That's* what I want."

"Okay. But I'll be down the way should you change your mind."

Bobby pulled up a chair and sat down next to his dead uncle. Roy had other fish to fry. One with a lot of money.

CHAPTER EIGHTEEN

Lawton reached for the pink-gold Dupont cigarette lighter on Mrs. Johnson's bedside table. He lit up and blew out a long stream of smoke that rolled into a big lazy cloud that drifted toward the ceiling and out onto the terrace where a servant dressed in black, white apron, no makeup, hair stuffed in a bun, was busy setting the brunch table.

Mrs. Johnson opened the bathroom door. Lawton stared at his future wife. Age, in its greedy way, had already picked the best parts. He wondered how he had made love to her. Despite the fizz in her eye, fulfillment at a certain age could be regressive, but Lawton hadn't lost sight of the servants, yachts, country clubs, the sweeping apartment in the Rive Gauche. The snug-as-a-bug winter chalet in the Swiss Alps, where guests skied down the slope for *petit déjeuner,* or that cozy farm in Èze Village just off the Grande Corniche that overlooked her other house in Saint-Jean-Cap-Ferrat that nipped the Mediterranean; but most important, Mrs. Johnson's endless supply of money, leather, and precious metal that she kept around like pennies in a bowl. Lawton turned to the old

1960s photo on the night table, where Leyland and Kathy, in foxhunting attire, sat astride Appaloosas with a pack of beagles barking at their hocks. She held the reins the way a good liar holds the truth: softly and without fear. She had a queen's eye that denied you were ever there and that sense of entitlement that doesn't mellow with time. Mrs. Johnson, back under the covers, whinnied like a filly, but Lawton's mind was now on Audrey and the day he had first met her on a Florida beach after he and Roy had returned from the first Gulf War. He was thinking of how she had smiled yet kept her distance. Allowed him to speak, but not deeply. Took his questions. Answered only those she chose. Accepted compliments but deflected advances. They enjoyed each other's company the way strangers on a train may share a laugh or the irony of their situation. When he told Audrey that she was beautiful, she let him know that it was an observation, not a conclusion. He was careful to look only at her eyes, avoid the deeper, more troublesome areas, but he wanted her so much he could barely keep his composure. He was fearful he might say the wrong thing, give the wrong impression, or that she might see him as someone who had already reached his limits. At bottommost, he was worried they weren't connecting. That she was already tired of him. They reached a vacant stretch of sand and sat down. Audrey wanted to float away. Be like the cloud up in the sky. Mrs. Johnson leaned over. "What are you thinking, Lawton?"

"Nothing," his eye up on that cloud.

Audrey said, "How long are you on leave?" As she unclasped her top and leaned into the deep white sand.

"I'm just out of the army."

"Were you in Iraq?"

"Yes."

"Was it bad?"

"Ugly."

"What do you plan on doing now?"

Lawton had no idea except that he didn't want to look at her topless. He didn't want to have to feel those things.

"My friend Roy and I are looking for work."

"Where y'all from?"

"Alabama. Roy, Mississippi."

"Where in Alabama?"

"Bibb County."

Audrey said, "I'm from Madison."

"Guess we're neighbors."

"Not walking distance."

"What brings you to Florida?"

Audrey wiped the sand off her face. "The surfing. I love the water."

"There's surfing in Madison?"

"No, silly. I live on a horse farm. I spend the summer here surfing and swimming. I want to do something that concerns the water. You're a good swimmer."

"Rangers are good at anything."

"I think you're going to miss the army."

"No. The army owns you. Tells you what to do."

Audrey saw a couple approaching. It was Roy and Roberta holding hands for the first time. As Roy waved, Audrey shut her eyes and drifted into the heat of the day. The ocean, one big doze. The wind heavy with brine and rattling voices. The swaying dune grass and kites full with the loneliness of youth when it's unsure about love.

Lawton got out of Mrs. Johnson's bed and drifted toward the terrace. He stepped out into the big Florida heat and put his phone to his ear.

Roy said, "Tonight is on."

"Where are you now?"

"My new bungalow at Surfside Colony. You know how to get here?"

"Yeah."

"Stop by at five. Bungalow 20. Just a few down from Audrey."

"I've gotta get rid of Kathy first."

"Just be here by five, so we can have a few words before I head out to make the incoming tide."

Mrs. Johnson stepped out onto the terrace. "Who's on the phone?"

Lying, "Julia."

"I thought she wasn't talking to you."

Lawton dropped the call. "Something came up."

"Let me speak to her."

"I don't think this is the time."

"Give me the phone."

"I can't."

"*Give* it to me, Lawton."

"She's not your daughter."

"As far as she's concerned, you're not her father."

"How would you know?"

"From everything you've told me." Mrs. Johnson headed back into the bedroom to get dressed and at a quicker pace than normal. "It makes me feel dirty to know that Julia has to work in a sex club." And with the sternness of a schoolmistress, "I'm going to do something about it."

"I'd appreciate you staying out of my business, Kathy."

Mrs. Johnson corrected him, "Now that we're getting married, your business *is* my business."

Lawton was hearing the warden, first day.

CHAPTER NINETEEN

That afternoon, Audrey, Julia, and Crystal leaped into the sky and sat in the vast empty air as if they were on thrones. Their arms extending up over their heads. Their knees high to maintain their position in the slot of rushing air. They tilted forward, joined hands, and like bolts of lightning flashed down to earth in a controlled spin. Crystal broke away first. Then Julia. Her proud mama next. Their canopies popping out like colored silk from a magician's hat as they drifted down to earth like feathers. Landing like birds on a wire. Laughing as if there were no tomorrow.

Roy's bungalow. Wanda violently swept a broom at Roy. "I'm *not* jumping out of airplanes."

"That's what a static line's for," Roy said. "You get pushed out. Chute automatically opens. The girls wanted you there."

"They *free*-fall. They *don't* jump from a static line."

"I thought you knew nothing about jumping."

"I did an art series about the world free-falling, and I used the metaphor of jumping as the modern existential dilemma."

"*Huh?*"

Looking at him like he was an idiot, "Those who free-fall and the rest of us stuck on the static line."

"You make any money?"

"That's the only thing you think about, Roy, is *money*," pushing him away with the end of the broom, not letting on about all the wealthy art collectors who made her a millionaire, many times over, buying her art that had to be explained to them by art advisors who knew how to diffuse the insecurity that wealth brings to people who bring nothing else with them. Wanda plumped up another couch pillow. "And I don't want to talk about this any further."

"What're you so angry for?"

"Because you *won't* drop the subject, Roy."

"I'm just trying to have a talk with you."

She aimed the broom at him. "You're making me sound like I'm a sissy, and I'm *not*."

"I never said you was a sissy."

"*Were* a sissy."

"Huh?"

Wanda hissed, "You can get *killed* skydiving."

"You can get killed doing a lot of things."

"That's not the point, Roy. I've done a lot of crazy things that take guts and courage."

"Sure you have."

"I *don't* like the way you said that."

Backing away from her, "There you go again."

"There *you* go again," aiming the broom handle at him.

"I think you got a problem, Wanda."

Poking him hard with the broom, "No, *you* got a problem."

"Look Wanda—"

"If you think coming down here on a moment's notice didn't take guts, something's wrong with you. Here I am trying to help you make this bungalow livable, and all you do is give me abuse."

"Coming down here is business."

"It still takes guts."

Roy said, "Business is for money. Skydiving is for fun. Or don't you like having any?"

Wanda shut the bedroom door. Ten long minutes later, Roy cautiously entered. Wanda was sitting in a chair by the bedroom window facing the beach. Her bare long legs up on the sill. Beer bottle sweat rings on her white tank top. She said, "The way you talked to Bobby. Pushing your movie. His uncle having just died. I expected more of you."

"I'm sorry."

"Bobby's my boyfriend."

"What're you doing here if he's your boyfriend?"

"Teaching him a lesson."

"*What* lesson?"

"*Look*, I resent you thinking I'm a sissy."

"I said it before, Wanda. I'll say it again. I do not think you're a sissy."

"I can do anything."

"Of course you can."

"I'm very brave."

"Except for skydiving."

This time she left the bungalow and almost knocked Lawton over.

Roy dragged him inside. "I was beginning to think you wasn't gonna show up."

"Kathy insisted on coming along. We had a bit of an argument. She's used to having her own way."

Roy looked down the road. "You didn't bring her?"

"Hell no."

"Good. Come on inside."

Lawton, looking back, "Who's the girl?"

"Long story," as Roy shut the door on Wanda, who was more than a little curious about the good-looking redneck.

Five minutes later Roy left the bungalow and bumped into the little sneak hiding in the doorway. Roy said to Lawton, "I'll get us some Chinese. Be right back." Then to Wanda, "Y'all can get to know each other in the meantime." Roy whispered to Lawton, now outside, "Ronnie's club don't close till three, so you got time, but the tide's coming in, so I gotta go."

Lawton said, "Where's the raft?"

"Right outside on the lawn." Handing Lawton a diagram, "The security alarms at the club are marked in red. All you gotta do is enter the numbers. The safe is in the office just to the side of Roberta's desk. Looks like a big old tricked-out cabinet dresser."

Lawton said, "You got the keys to the truck?"

Roy handed them to him.

Lawton turned back to the bungalow, "What's her story?"

"One of them girls always got you under scrutiny. Good hunting, brother." Roy headed down to the beach. He pushed the raft out to sea and swam with it over the first few big waves. Then he started up the motor and headed to Sailfish Point.

Wanda was inside waiting in the big chair for Lawton to walk over and come on to her. He politely said hello, sat down, and kept to himself. His quiet country manner and tumbleweed good looks were getting to her. She thought he had the rural habits of a man on the dole who hoboed until dusk then found the nearest tree and settled in for the night. Lawton pulled a paperback from his hip pocket and started to read. Insulted by the hobo's inattention, Wanda went to the bedroom and slammed the door.

A short nap turned into a knockout. Later that evening, she drifted out of the bedroom and let out a big wide yawn. "What time is it?" Lawton tossed her the iPhone that was on the coffee table. She brought it close to her still-sleepy eyes. "*Midnight?*" And flopped down on the armchair next to Lawton, who was spread out on the couch. This time the hobo was going to pay attention. She poked him with her foot. "*Hey.*"

Lawton barely looked up.

She said, "Where's the food?"

"Huh?"

"Chinese, Roy said he was bringing."

"It's coming," turning a page of his book.

"*Coming?* Roy left yesterday." She stared at the big iced pitcher on the coffee table. Then at the hobo on the couch who seemed so still inside she thought he was dead. "Where the hell did he go? Mott Street?"

"Car broke down."

Wanda yawned and reached into the pretzel bag next to Lawton. She got a handful of crumbs stuck in her nails. "You saved nothing for me."

"Roy'll be back any minute."

Tossing the bag away. "Why're you so mean to me?"

"I'm not mean."

Wondering why he wouldn't even turn his head her way. "You act like I'm the most awful person on earth."

"Maybe you are," smiling.

"Maybe *you* are," not smiling. "What's in that thing over there?"

Lawton moved the pitcher toward her. "Spiked lemonade."

She poked her nose inside. "I get drunk real fast."

"Drink slowly."

"Doesn't make a difference. There's something wrong with me."

"You're dying?"

"*No.* Something to do with my something," and poured herself a cup. She pushed Lawton's legs over and sat down Indian style on the couch. Cup in drinking position like it was a sleepover party. She took several big gulps and then drank it all.

"Easy on the booze, lady."

"*Easy shmeezy,*" she sang and offered him a sip. "Go ahead. I don't have a disease."

"No, thanks. What's your name again?"

"Wanda. Wanda Morris Herman; and *don't* call me Wanda Morris the Cat. I hate it." She rolled an ice cube over her lips and stared at the good-looking redneck. "Roy told me you sat in a prison for ten years."

"You and Roy a couple now?"

"Depends."

"On what?"

Shoving a pillow behind her, "How I feel at the moment, which is quite tipsy."

"Y'all move pretty fast."

"*Yawwwll*," throwing her head back and howling with laughter. "Do people in the South really talk like that?"

"That's how we speak."

"I wish we spoke like that. I heard myself, once, and swore I'd never listen to myself again." Taking another sip. Eyeballing Lawton the way a kid does when her parents bring home someone new instead of the same old neighborhood bore. "Must've been hard."

"What?"

"Prison."

"Let's not talk about it."

"How long were you on death row?"

"I *wasn't* on death row. You gonna drink that whole thing?"

Wanda stared into the pitcher on the coffee table and wondered if she could.

Lawton said, "Somebody was over here, before, looking for Bobby."

Wanda made a tight face. "I don't want to talk about him."

"I took a walk over to where he was supposed to be, and an old woman fired a gun at me thinking I was Bobby and hit the neighbor's bungalow instead. Now she's down at the police station. Say they're gonna let her go because of that Stand Your Ground law;

how she thought I was going to harm her. I'd let your friend Bobby know to stay away from her."

"Bobby threw her out. That's why."

"Want a napkin?"

"Nope," sneezing anyway. "Everybody's gun crazy around here. Maybe I'll get a gun."

"Don't."

Wanda touched his arm as if it might sting her. "One of those prison gang tattoos?"

"I wouldn't know."

Her tipsy eyes were on the holy cross with death skulls pierced at each end. She took a photo of it with her iPhone.

Lawton said, "You're gonna get a tattoo?"

"Nope," dropping her voice, letting him know she meant business. "You know those dates you go out on when you want something to happen and nothing happens?"

"Yeah."

"I feel like I'm on one of them," taking another big gulp. Feeling the booze in her head, "You've never heard of me?"

"Who?"

"*Me*. Wanda Morris Herman."

Lawton said, "You're spilling your drink on me."

She spilled it the other way. "I'm famous."

"Nice to meet you. I'm Lawton."

"*Hey*. I'm serious."

"So am I."

Wanda said, "I'm on all the party A-lists."

"So am I."

"Never seen you anywhere," losing her balance.

"You're spilling your drink all over me."

"I'm sorry."

"I'm *all* wet."

"*Sorry!*" Wanda drank up the rest. "I'm hungry. I just bought a farmhouse near where Jackson Pollock used to live, and I wish I was there, not here, waiting for a bucket of Chinese food. Maybe I'll climb the palm tree outside and get us a coconut."

"Go ahead."

"You don't even know who he is."

"Who *who* is?"

"Pollock," swinging her arms back to make a ponytail.

"Who is he?"

"Some guy got drunk one night and crashed into a tree," picking up her empty cup. Refilling it. Her ponytail falling apart. "I got a view of Accabonac Harbor right from my bedroom window. Wish I were there now." Crossing her arms and confessing, "I'm too impulsive."

"You are?"

"That's my new problem."

"What's your old problem?"

"Too shy. I grew up youngest of five kids."

"That's nice."

"No, it wasn't. I was end of the litter, and so my parents were already burnt out from having four other kids. I was like that unopened letter at the bottom of the pile that should've been opened months ago," brushing her hair away, so she could see.

"Where's this farmhouse?"

"The Springs. But you don't care."

"About what?"

"My problems," Wanda said.

"Oh, I care. Where's the Springs? I've never heard of it."

"My Hamptons summer retreat. Don't you *ever* get out?"

"I just did," meaning prison.

"Well—Maybe I'll invite you up one weekend that is if you don't turn out to be like most guys who are mental."

"How far away is it?"

Pointing north, "Long Island. I got it cheap for four and a half mill."

"*Dollars?*"

"Yeah. The banker who owned it took a beating. Hated wild turkeys and living on a farm. I love it. It extends out to the bay. When the sun goes down, everything turns golden. When it rises, everything turns golden. My farmhouse faces east and west. The birds fly north and south. I wish I were in love."

Lawton said, "*Four* and a half million dollars?"

"You're not listening to me."

"I'm listening, all right."

"I want a love that doesn't turn into a routine. Something so intense that nothing ever matters. And I don't mean romantic love. I'm talking about full-throttle in-your-face love. Otherwise I'm gonna go nuts," reaching out her arms to grab hold of the couch. "I think I drank too much."

"You really have that much money, or are you one of them girls who likes to make up things?"

"I got *tons* of money, mister."

"I don't believe you."

"I don't care what you believe."

"What are you famous for?"

"Using disguises to experience the loss of identity from the feminine perspective and all that hooey. I got the MacArthur genius award."

"For doing what?"

"For being a genius, silly."

"You're a genius?"

"—Probably not, but museums all over the world request my work now, and all the rich people buy it. My minimum price starts at half a mill. I mean, I'll negotiate if *yawwwll* buy more'n one piece," throwing her head back and howling with laughter. "I like to laugh."

"I can tell."

"You're okay."

"Thanks. You're not so bad yourself."

"I'm invited to all the art galas and events, and I get driven there by limousine. How 'bout you?"

"I gotta walk."

"Too bad. I got more pillows on one couch than you ever slept on in your whole life and I'm doing great, except in the boy department."

"Ever been married?"

"Yeah, to a dope addict. Shows ya what a dope I am."

"You're not a dope. I like you. I like you a whole lot."

"Thanks, mister. I like you, too. I think there's something about you. I don't know you. That's probably why. Once you get to know someone, they can be a real pain in the neck."

"Ya think?"

"Yup, and if I end up on my deathbed with all my money and fame and say: *For whom did I live?* And there's no one lover or child to say: *For me.* That's fine with me."

"Well, don't worry. If I weren't in love with the girl next store, I'd be in love with you."

"Now you're lying."

Lawton said, "You're crazy."

"Thirty million dollars crazy."

"You're full of baloney."

"Ya think so?" Wanda took the only magazine off the coffee table. "This is the most prestigious design magazine in the world," opening it up. "It's hot off the press," and put it in Lawton's face. "You're looking at a six-page feature of my Paris apartment all fixed up. Here's a photo of me in my blue booties at the front door."

"I thought you lived in New York."

"I'm talking about *Paris.*"

"You're French?"

"*Hell* no. I'm from Detroit."

"Then what're you doing here?"

"Getting drunk."

"Why?"

"I don't know why."

"I thought you was on your way to Paris."

"That's next week. I'm having a big splash and can't wait. I got eight large rooms in the prettiest eighteenth-century Rive Gauche mansion with vaulted ceilings and windows so tall the sun has to climb inside. Not a dump like this where I'm stuck talking to Slim Pickens."

Lawton said, "I thought we was pals. Now you're being rude."

"Who *isn't* rude when you're drunk? *Isn't* that the whole point?"

"You speak French?"

"I don't have to. All I have to do is point and *ka-ching*!"

"Point at what?"

"At whatever I want and all the fashion designers give me their stuff to wear at all the big galas for nothing, unlike *you* and your Roy Rogers outfit," tugging at his cowboy shirt like it was thrift material. "My pal Catherine Deneuve—that old French movie actress, in case ya don't know who she is *either!*—would laugh her Guccis off at you."

"What's wrong with Roy Rogers?"

"Geezuz, even my parrot dresses better than you and all he's got are feathers." Looking down at Lawton as if he were at the bottom of a well and ready to leave him there. She growled, "I suppose ya wanna wait *another* ten years?"

"For you to speak French?"

"No."

"For what then?"

"*Whaddya* think?" Looking into his eyes, wondering if he could add one and one.

Lawton held Wanda up as straight as he could. "This is what I think, Miz Queen Bee of the Art World," wiping away the dribble on her chin. Looking into her deep, pretty blue eyes that swam of far-off visions that almost made him forget Audrey. "It's not fair sleeping with a drunk girl."

"Then you've never seen *Girls Gone Wild*," reaching for the lamp. Knocking it over. The light going out, including hers. Lawton took Wanda Morris the Cat off the floor and put her to bed. On his way out the bungalow, he saw Audrey ride down the dirt path on her matte-black Monster. He almost went her way. Instead, he headed toward the truck. It was time to open a safe.

CHAPTER TWENTY

Ronnie Harrison's Sailfish Point mansion faced the Atlantic with a permanent stare. The master bedroom swapped light, high and low, from an eighty-inch widescreen. The rest of the house was dark except the kitchen, which was muted by soft counter lights, but all Roy could think of, as he drifted ashore, was whether Lawton would choke and head home. He had called earlier that day and said, "I been thinking things over, Roy."

Roy, tired of all the thinking. "You used to never be this way, son."

"Well, why is it that I'm outta prison and still feel like I'm in it?"

"'Cause ya got no money."

Lawton got deep. "Wouldn't it be nice to live in a world without money."

Roy reminded him, "You already do."

Roy hid the raft in a clump of wild grass where the rising tide stained the beach. He stayed wide of the pool and went around the north side of the mansion where the den faced the driveway, but something downwind overtook his senses. It was foul, unwashed. At first, Roy thought it was coming from the pool deck. Then he saw the bruise at the far end of the patio. It weighed in at 250 hundred pounds. An anthology of tattoos raveled up its arms. A wide black bandana swathed its forehead. Roy was thinking of all the houses he and Lawton had taken down; never once did they run into a fellow traveler, let alone a biker, who was now saying to the woman by his side, "You think he's from outta space?" Not too sure why the tall man dressed in black from head to toe was heading their way.

The woman, in jeans and black engineer boots, said, "You oughta ask him where he thinks you're from, Hank."

Hank beaded his gun on the man in black, "Who the fuck're you?"

Roy was more interested in the woman. She looked familiar in the margin of house light. He tried to place her, but she had been accessorized with years of bad teeth and a long, yellow, hollow face that grieved of drugs. The woman said, "Hank, you said this was gonna be easy."

Hank, even dumber than he looked, "How did I know a big frog from Mars was gonna show up?" Then to Roy, "Who the fuck are you?"

Roy trying to deescalate the situation. "Friend, why don't you put that gun down for a moment?"

"Whyn't ya get the fuck outta here?"

"I will, but mind if I give y'all a little friendly tip first?"

Hank said, "Fuck off, asshole."

Roy opened his hands to show that he wasn't a threat. "Well, before I do, what y'all wanna do is work y'all way to the point that when y'all do tell me to get the fuck outta here, there'll be no reason for me to disagree. See, you fire that gun now and kill me, I'm still here. Think about that, Hank."

The woman nudged him. "He's not all wrong."

Hank turned to the woman and wondered aloud if maybe she had a thing for him.

She said, "You ever see me with a black dude?"

"Maybe I haven't been looking hard enough."

"Hank, you shoot him, we'll never get that bike worth fifty grand. All you'll do is wake up the whole neighborhood, while we run ass backward outta here."

Hank said to Roy, "The bike is mine. Try the next house."

"You can have the bike."

"Good. Get outta here."

"When the time is right, Hank."

"The time is right—*now*."

"The time is right when we both get what we want," Roy said. "We use our heads, that'll happen."

The woman, more than a little curious. "You trying to make a deal with us?"

"That I am."

The woman stepped forward. "What's the deal?"

"We both take down this house."

"At the *same* time?"

Roy said, "That would be imprudent."

She came a little closer. "You look familiar."

"So do you."

She said, "Years ago there were these cat burglars. Never carried a gun. Always polite. Took 'em four minutes to get in and out of a house. One was about your height and married to a Roberta LaHood. I used to pole dance with her. She was in tight with the boss, and if you didn't treat her like the Queen of Sheba, she made your life miserable."

Roy wanted to tell her she wasn't all that wrong, but he saw Clarice in the bedroom window holding an icepack over her nose. A mobile phone to her ear. A glass in her hand. She swallowed something and walked away.

The woman, staring at the window. "I wouldn't mind living in a house like that, Hank."

"You wouldn't know what to do in there."

"You're right, Hank. After living in a sleeping bag with you for eight years, it would be a whole new experience."

"I can't steal you a house."

"Why don't you try?" The woman looked at him the way she looked at her life: hard and going nowhere. She said to Roy, "All right. You go in first. I wanna see how good you are. But you got four minutes. That's all. Then we go in for the bike."

Roy said, "Fair enough. By the way, what's your name?"

"Dee."

"*Dee Culver?*"

"Yeah. Better hurry up."

Clarice was on the kitchen floor, holding her phone to her ear, picking up all the ice cubes that had popped out of the ice tray. She was waiting for Ronnie to get back with the Vicodin that the attending ER physician had prescribed for her pain. Ronnie said, "Call me one more time, I'm throwing it all out the window."

Roy entered the house through the den window. He didn't need to disable the alarm. Crystal had let him know that it was never turned on while someone was home. He went down the hall and found the basement door and went down the stairway. It opened to a massive bare white room with an unfinished wet bar. There were no windows. Deep in the corner, between the wet bar and back counter, under what looked like a white birdcage cover, was the safe where all the cash was put at the end of the month before Ronnie tooted off to Antigua.

Roy beamed his Leopold on the safe's dial. He worked it full to the left, once to the right, back left, half right home and then to thirty-eight. He put his hand on the extending side lever. Just a push and it opened like a company demonstration, but the feeling he got was like looking at a beautiful woman undressed for the first time. He placed all the bills into a double-strap top-loading waterproof duffel bag. What he couldn't take he left: small bills, Miami Heat tickets (before and after LeBron). The diamond bracelets and unset stones took the trip. Then he sealed the safe door with epoxy. He didn't want Ronnie to find the safe empty so quickly. He wanted him to stew. It was then that Roy remembered that he had forgotten to tell Lawton to do the same thing.

On his way up, Roy noticed that the kitchen counter lights had been turned off. He heard what seemed to be a crash coming from an upstairs TV. The sound of splintered gunfire spread throughout the house. Roy slipped through the library window and hurried past the pool, where Dee and Hank should've been waiting. He checked his watch. Five minutes: a little rusty. Roy heard another shot, the kind that echoes in the open air. The lights turned on in the mansion. A man was walking up a flight of stairs, one arm longer than the other. Roy loaded the duffel bag into the raft and pushed it out to sea.

CHAPTER TWENTY-ONE

Ronnie Harrison looked dazed, as if someone had spun him around like a top and let him go. His Glock .45 hanging in his right hand. The Vicodins in his left. Clarice shifted her eyes from the widescreen mounted on the wall and hit the mute button. "You got the goddamn painkillers?"

Ronnie dropped into a big white leather chair and let the words run off his tongue. "I got a bit of a problem."

Clarice said, "You will if you don't gimme them goddamn pain killers," aiming the remote at him as she crawled across the king-size bed.

Ronnie tossed the vial. She caught it like Buster Posey. Ronnie said, "See, I was just coming home," his eyes up toward the ceiling, dull and heavy with the moment, "and I thought she was back."

"Who?" Swallowing two Vicodins.

"You know."

"No, I don't know," reading the prescription label.

"Roberta."

"*Hey*, why do they say two every six hours? What if I'm in pain every two hours? The hell am I suppose to do, Ronnie?" Clarice counted the pills. "They don't think somebody can be in pain every two hours?"

Ronnie said, "It was loud. *Really* loud."

Clarice, staring at the Glock, wondering if the reason he had taken so long was that he had stopped off at the gun range. "What was loud?"

Ronnie floated by like a blowfish.

"You haven't been taking that new shit Marty's been handing out, Ronnie? Everybody's bitchin' on it."

Ronnie said, "So, the fat guy says," seeing Hank right before him. His black bandana over his head like goth mourning crêpe, "Where's the fucking Harley?" Turning to Clarice. "I don't even own a Harley. Then he looks at my brand-new Ducati and tells me it's a fag bike."

"What are you talking about, Ronnie?"

"The fat guy."

"*What* fat guy?"

"Holding the gun."

"*What* gun?"

"Guy in the garage," Ronnie now facing it.

"*What* garage?"

"I was aiming at him."

"*Who?*"

"The biker."

"*What* biker?"

"And killed her."

"*Ronnie*. Did you get stoned at the gun club again?"

Ronnie's eyes on the floor. Then up at the ceiling. Clarice not sure if he wasn't sleepwalking. Ronnie walked around the bedroom like a first-time home buyer. "I was aiming for his head."

"*Whose* head?"

Ronnie, closer to the window. Looking down at the blue irises, which were violet under the garage lights. "It's not how I thought it would happen."

"How *what* would happen?"

"What *fucking* happened." Pointing. "There he is crying over her."

"*Who* is?"

"The fat guy."

Clarice up on her toes. One hand protecting her broken nose. She took a long look out the window. "You *shot* her?"

Ronnie shrugged. "The whole thing happened so fast. I don't know what I shot."

"Ronnie, the hell happened down there?"

"It's not my fault."

"Well, whosoever it was, you better call the police."

"Nothing but trouble you call them."

"Ronnie, there's a *dead* person down there."

"They tried to rob me, Clarice. He put a gun on me."

"*Call* the police, Ronnie."

"I don't think so."

"You don't, I will." Clarice reached for the phone.

Ronnie pulled it out of her hand. "I'll take care of this."

He went downstairs through the kitchen door to the garage and tapped Hank on the shoulder. Hank looked up. His face a blur. Then he backed off his knees and landed flat and heavy as if he'd been thrown off a truck. Ronnie walked over to the gardening shelf against the wall and wiped off his shooting hand. He called 911 and said, "I just stood my ground."

CHAPTER TWENTY-TWO

Morning. Glorious sunshine. Birds a cappella. All Julia had to do was get dressed in clothing she didn't like, ride down to the university campus, do the interview, make a good impression, and become a college student for the fall *if* she could meet the financial requirements, but when she arrived at the school, the interviewing professor's office was shut, possibly sealed. His absorbed work-study aide said he would be back shortly.

Julia searched for a chair. She found a white plastic wire seat that looked more like a casualty of an earthquake than a piece of furniture and pushed it up against the cluttered printouts that were buried under piles of graded and ungraded papers, syllabi, handbooks, cups of old coffee, and the thick smell of student sweat, white-out, ink cartridges, and pencil lead that made the office look more like a cram session before finals.

Fifteen minutes later Julia asked the work-study, again, when Professor Soler would be arriving for the interview. She told Julia to take a seat and wait. Julia said, "I already have one," to which there was no response.

And it went on like this every fifteen minutes for the next two hours against the sound of computer keyboards, telephones, and the occasional cerebral sigh. A tall, ruler-thin man, wearing a Tattersall button-down shirt with researcher smudges, entered. He proceeded to the office at the end of the hall, the one Julia had thought had been sealed off from the world. He dropped off a packet of papers on the work-study's cubicle then closed the door to his chamber, which completed his separation from reality measured not in days nor hours, but in semesters, revisions, resubmissions, and extensions, all useless in the real world where things expire and rot. Julia approached the work-study, who was nibbling on a gluten-free banana muffin. "Was that Professor Soler who just walked by?"

The work-study didn't bother to look up from under her shrub of black tousled hair. "I already told you. He'll be here shortly."

"I was just wondering whether I'll be sleeping over."

"*Please*, sit down."

"You said that when I walked in two hours ago."

"I'll say it again."

"Look, I've been patiently waiting two hours, and unless I'm wrong, no one seems to care."

The work-study reached for her muffin. Julia stopped her hand. "Are you listening to me?"

The work-study rushed down the hall. A few moments later, she returned with the ruler-thin scholar gripping an open blue folder. He said to Julia, with the sternness and sanctity of someone on his way to tenure, "What's the issue here?"

Julia said, "I've been waiting two hours to see Mr. Soler."

The work-study corrected her. "*Professor* Soler."

The professor said, "You have an appointment with me?"

"More than two hours ago."

"Who are you?"

"Julia Gibbs."

The scholar glanced down at the blue folder with Julia's name on it. "Come with me."

The professor's office was surrounded with stacks of books, mostly borrowed and unreturned. He leaned back into his swivel chair and studied the blue file. Now and again he looked up at the open green file on his desk—the one with the recommendations, including Julia's part-time job as an honor-student researcher in a medical lab.

He said, "Your grades are excellent. Your teacher recommendations, superb. Your math and English SATs, more than impressive." Looking up. "But your little performance outside wasn't."

"Excuse me?"

"Your little performance."

"*What* little performance?"

The professor said, "The one with Melinda."

"Who's Melinda?"

"My work-study aide."

"What about her?"

"You were rude to her."

"She was rude to me."

"Melinda wasn't rude. She has a lot of work, notwithstanding her own studies."

"She was rude the moment I walked in."

"Melinda is never rude—overworked, yes, but never rude."

Julia said, "I don't think being overworked and rude are incompatible."

"Melinda is one of my best students. I've never seen her this upset, and I will not tolerate it."

"I apologize, sir, but I was under the impression I waited two hours to discuss my admission, not Melinda."

The professor was confident with his authority, even relishing the opportunity to exercise it. "You seem to miss the point, Ms. Gibbs."

"What point?"
"You threatened Melinda."
"*I* threatened Melinda?"
"You put your hand on her."
"I didn't *threaten* her."
"Did you put your hand on her?"
"I was trying to get her attention."
"You threatened her."
"I wanted to know what was keeping you."
"Why didn't you just speak to her?"
"I did more than once over two hours, and it had no effect."
"So you got physical?"
"*Physical?*"
"What you did was a violation."
"*What* was a violation?"

The professor, as if having to remind her. "Touching someone is a violation at this school unless you have permission. Had it not been for your impressive grades and my curiosity in meeting you, I'd have already had you thrown off campus."

Julia said, "Then you misunderstand."

"I do not misunderstand. You were aggressive. Aggression is a form of behavior we do not tolerate here, whether it is political as in the suppression of a people's rights or an individual's personal freedom. We do not tolerate aggression."

"Neither do I."
"Then why did you touch her?"
"I wanted to know what was detaining you."
"You wanted to control her."
"—This is getting dumb." Swiping a fly away.

It became still in the office.

Professor Soler said, "You think you're in a strip club?"

"*Excuse* me?"

"Maybe working in a strip club has given you the wrong impression about the rest of the world."

Wondering who this nut was. "How would you know I work in an entertainment-related business?"

"That's not the point."

"It is now," Julia said.

"I was using it as an example."

"What do you know about entertainment clubs?"

"You came here to interview me?"

"You know exactly why I came here."

"This interview has reached its conclusion."

Julia, not ready to go. "I didn't put anything in my application other than medical-lab work and surfing lessons."

"In full disclosure, you should have said something about your *other* work."

"I do enough of that Wednesday through Saturday."

"By not disclosing all activities outside your academic studies, Ms. Gibbs, you consciously left out the most important one, and I find that deceitful."

"Well *I* don't. I had to earn a living. When I get a higher education, I'll be able to do it in a less distracting way."

"Yes, but not in this university."

Julia, now at the door. "I had to wait two hours to find out you're an idiot. That's education enough."

CHAPTER TWENTY-THREE

Ronnie floated into the club office like a piece of bobbing driftwood. Roberta watched him from behind her granite desk. She said, "Two cops from homicide stopped by this morning, Ronnie." She pushed two police cards across the desk in case he was interested.

Ronnie searched for his watering can.

Roberta said, "I caught 'em hanging around the front entrance pressing their noses up against the glass door."

Ronnie stuck his head into a closet.

"I told 'em, 'Y'all a little early to see the show.' The big cop said they just wanted to have a chat, look around, ask a couple of questions, such as did I know Dee Culver and for how long—Ronnie, it's over *there*," pointing.

Ronnie found the watering can behind the coffee machine.

"They wanted to know about a certain Hank Kosinski. When I last saw him or Dee. Remember Dee Culver?"

Ronnie was now looking for the Sweet'N Low.

"So, the big cop says maybe there's something I'd like to tell him about Dee. So I tell him there's so many girls coming in and out of the club I'd need a search engine in my head to know who's who. They ask me, again, about this Hank Kosinski. Do I know him? Some biker–home invader who's got a long rap sheet. Beats up old people. I say, 'No, I don't know him.' Then they say Kosinski and Dee were into amphetamines, crack, heroin—any shit they can get their hands on. Do I know that right under my nose Marty Bannister, the bartender, is dealing drugs? I say to the big cop, one who thinks size means I have to tell him everything, 'If you got so much on Marty the bartender, why don't you arrest the son of a bitch.' He shrugs. Leaves. Say they'll keep in touch. Then I call you on your mobile phone, but you didn't pick up. So I try the house, and Clarice tells me you're taking a walk on the beach, thinking things over."

Ronnie poured some coffee but overshot the rim. Roberta hurried over and wiped up the mess. "Ronnie, you feeling okay?"

"Bill Moyers might be going off the air."

"So what? The morning news said the police was really glad you killed that biker. What I want to know is if they're so glad, how come I find two homicide cops snooping around?"

Ronnie said, "I'm gonna send a check to that guy on PBS with the suspenders, so he stops begging and puts Bill back on and pays him what he deserves. Call the gardener and tell him to get his ass over here."

Roberta, standing in front of Ronnie, hoping he would wake up soon, "Look, I think the police think you didn't tell 'em everything."

"They're just being cops."

"They're being more than that, Ronnie."

"You know the Stand Your Ground law?"

"Sure, what about it, Ronnie?"

"It means I can basically do what the fuck I want."

"Who told you that?"

"My lawyer."

"Well, I got news for you. I think you and Bill Moyers are both through."

Ronnie was now in his office, separated from Roberta by a sleek glass wall. He dropped into a big white leather chair and leaned all the way back as if a barber were about to shave him. Every once in a while, he breathed hard or blew his nose. Scratched his chin. Yawned. Regained focus. His face, unfortified by any inner activity, looked like a toy that had been unpacked, shelved, and ticketed for sale. If anything had happened the night before, it possessed him on lease with condition and allowance to come back when it pleased like that ghost who'd stopped by on a motorcycle for a little chat around four that morning. The ghost, in a cold hovering haze, had spoken these frosted words: *Tell Roy I should've listened to him.* Then puff. The apparition, gone. The bedroom, moments before filled with spectral glitter, was now muted in darkness and ventilation. Clarice had slept right through it, but Ronnie knew what he had seen. What he didn't know was if it had been real or caught between the possibilities of something beyond or something miscued from within. But he had seen something—even if he hadn't.

The few minutes Roberta had given Ronnie to adjust himself in his office were over. She grabbed the dailies off her desk and limped over with her sore foot to Ronnie's office and waited by his door under the shunting lights that squinted off the hi-tech glass-and-metal furniture. Her purple eyelid from her fall in her kitchen affected neither Ronnie's curiosity nor charity. Roberta, inches away from the slumbering bull, breeched the silence: "I've been going over the figures, Ronnie. We're sixteen percent off liquor this month even though we went through the same number of bottles the month before. And I know why."

Ronnie's head was like a balloon in the air. "You talking to me?"

"I don't know, Ronnie. You tell me."

He shifted his beached weight. "What's with Marty?"

"That's what I'm talking about."

Ronnie said, "Police say he's been dealing drugs?"

"Didn't we just discuss that?"

"He's gonna get busted tonight."

"Who's gonna get busted, Ronnie?"

"Dumbbell Marty."

"*Where?*"

Ronnie said, "You wanna be there?"

"I'd *love* to be there. You set it up with the police?"

"Set what up?"

"The bust."

"*I'm* gonna fucking bust him."

"Oh you always say that, Ronnie. Then you do nothing."

"Think I'm joking?"

"Look, y'all grew up together."

"So what?"

"Ronnie, every time you get lonesome, you hit the bottle with him and talk old times, which is at least once a week in the backroom bar."

"Not anymore."

"Look, Ronnie—"

"*Not* anymore."

"About what happened last night—"

"This is the last time, Roberta. I don't care how far we go back or how Marty's related to my cousin Barbara. This time Marty's finished." Ronnie leaned back. Let out air. He touched the edge of his desk to keep himself balanced. "Fucking dumbbell Marty. The moron goes to Greece on his honeymoon and takes his basketball, so he can do lay-ups in the morning. Unbelievable. The Parthenon is a block away, and this moron thinks it's March Madness."

"His wife didn't complain."

"Roberta, you go to Athens, you think maybe there's something else besides basketball?"

"It was *his* honeymoon."

"I love the way he paws his upper lip over his lower and tells you how he coulda gone pro if he were just a little taller. How 'bout three feet taller?"

"Anything else you and the police work out?"

Ronnie stared at Roberta. "What's it to you?"

"I don't know. It's been kind of quiet around here since you shot those two."

"It's one o'clock in the afternoon. It better be quiet." He reached into his desk and found a lollipop.

"Maybe you oughta go home, Ronnie. Chill out. Give yourself a few days' rest. Give the *whole* thing some rest. Look, I spoke to Clarice," touching him, so he'd turn her way. "She told me you murdered those two. Is that true, Ronnie?"

"She's an idiot."

"Did you really murder Dee and that Kosinski?"

"Is that what Roy did?"

"What?"

"Go home. Chill out?"

"When?"

"When he shot your boy toy, Raydel Palmero."

"Roy went to jail."

"Did he see something?"

"See what?"

"You tell me."

"Ronnie, *what're* you talking about?"

"There's a lot to see out there."

"Out *where?*"

"Where there are ghosts."

"You saw a *ghost?*"
"Yeah, Hank Kosinski."
"You saw *him* or a *ghost?*"
"I'm asking if Roy saw a ghost."
"I don't think so."
"That kid," Ronnie said.
"Which one?"
"One Roy shot: Raydel Palmero."
"What about him?"
"Ever show up at the foot of your bed?"
"All the time."
"No kidding."
"Until he was shot."
"Ohhh."
Roberta said, "Roy didn't see a ghost and neither did you."
"How would you know?"
"There *are* no ghosts."
"Then what the fuck did I see?"
"It was your imagination, Ronnie."
"Or your lack of it. You think he's gonna try and kill me?"
Roberta, shuffling the spreadsheets together. "*Who's* gonna kill you?"
"Your husband. He killed your last lover."
"Raydel had it coming, Ronnie, but if Roy's gonna kill you, there's nothing you can do about it."
Ronnie turned around, lifted his shirt, and showed her his Glock. "You wanna bet?"
Roberta thought he looked goofy with the gun in his waistband and the lollipop bulging in his cheek. She got up off his desk. "Ronnie, you got lucky last night. You're gonna need more than luck you wanna kill Roy."
"Maybe that's what I want him to think."

"Then tell Roy you saw a ghost. You won't have to kill him. He'll die laughing."

Ronnie disagreed, "The ghost said, 'I should have listened to Roy.'"

Roberta said, "Maybe he should have," and left the office.

CHAPTER TWENTY-FOUR

Clarice leaned over the second-floor bannister and shouted, "Why do you lock up everything?"

Ronnie walked up the stairs and went right past her.

She followed him into the bedroom then into his walk-in closet and took the outdated Miami Vice espadrilles out of his hands. "How the hell am I supposed to get dressed tonight with everything locked up in your safe."

Ronnie said, "Why did you tell Roberta I murdered two people?"

"I didn't say 'murder.'"

"Roberta said you did," reaching for his other favorite shoes.

"Fuck Roberta. She'll do or say anything to destroy our relationship."

"Who else have you been talking to?"

"No one, Ronnie, but they're gonna know you blew Hank away."

"And just how're they gonna know?"

"Forensics, Ronnie."

"They sent a forensic team over?"

"No. But if they *do*, you're fucked."

"Clarice, I stood my ground. They send anybody over, it'll be to shake my hand."

"Sure, Ronnie, but Hank was in distress and in no shape to do anything other than grieve. You didn't have to kill him." Taking the shirt out of Ronnie's hand. "You're wearing blue. Blue don't go with brown."

Ronnie said, "The police were sure glad I shot that son of a bitch."

"I suppose they told you."

"It's something they been wanting to do a long time. Now all the pensioners in the trailer parks don't have to go on lockdown every night."

"Police glad you shot the girl too?"

Looking for his shoehorn. "I *told* you. I *missed*."

"Ronnie, you shot her right in the heart. You call that a miss?"

Crawling on the floor. "Where's my shoehorn, Clarice?"

She put the shoehorn in front of his nose. "Why did you kill her?"

"Look, Clarice, I've had a long day."

"*Why* did you fucking kill her?"

Standing up, brushing himself off. "You ever kill somebody?"

"Only in my mind."

"Believe me, when a situation happens, you don't know what the fuck you're shooting."

"She didn't have a gun."

"I missed. *How* many times I have to tell you? He shot. Then I shot. She's dead."

"I'm sure he'd say you shot *then* he shot."

"Clarice, this is *my* home. I can shoot whenever the fuck I want. I don't have to wait my turn. And stop being a goddamn lawyer. Just because you dated Buford doesn't mean you're a legal scholar."

"They could say you shot without cause."

"They tried to *rob* me, Clarice. That's cause enough," looking for his dress socks, pulling out every drawer. "I'll say one thing. That son of a bitch Hank was scared, and I thought ghosts were supposed to be the ones who were scary."

Clarice stepped back. "What're you talking about?"

"A ghost." Looking for his belt.

"You're talking about a ghost or Hank?"

"Both."

"*Ronnie—*"

"What?"

"I think you should watch *Paranormal State* if you saw a ghost."

Finding a belt he had lost months ago. "Paranormal *what?*"

"Show on TV. There was this one episode—" Opening her dresser top drawer. Scattering everything in it. "*Hey.* Where's that necklace, Ronnie? You lock that up too?"

"It's where it belongs."

"It belongs *here.*"

"It belongs in my safe."

"I told you I wanted to wear it tonight."

"You don't need a necklace."

"Everybody stares at me when I wear it, Ronnie."

"You like people staring at you?"

Clarice crossed her arms and blocked his way into the bathroom. "I want that necklace or else I'm leaving."

"What's with this TV show?"

"*Get* me the necklace."

"I *told* you. It's in the safe, where it belongs."

"*Get* it."

"What's this TV show, Clarice?"

"Get me the fucking necklace, first." Heading downstairs.

"Where're you going?"

"To the safe."

Following her. "Did this show happen to be about ghosts?"

On their way down the big grand stairway. "Yeah."

"Is it on now?"

"No, but they got reruns *all* the time, Ronnie."

Stopping her halfway down. "You want the goddamn necklace? You tell me about this show."

"It's all about ghosts."

"They come at four in the morning?"

"Hell do I know when they come, but they exist. Now, I want that necklace."

"You believe in that stuff?"

Trying to walk around him. "You said you saw a ghost."

"Yeah, well, I saw something."

"All I know there's people can talk to Hank if they want. Maybe they can tell you what this Roy LaHood was really up to."

"What if Hank tells some psychic that he didn't have his gun in his hand?"

"Ronnie—in a court of law, who's gonna believe a ghost?"

Ronnie almost laughed.

"Open the safe."

He pulled off the safe cover. Squatted. Turned the combination. Gave the handle a tug. Then another tug. Then he talked to the safe man-to-man: "Hey, we've done this before," and tried the combination, again, but it wouldn't budge.

Clarice said, "You forget the combination?"

"I know it like I know my birthday."

Clarice lit a cigarette on an empty stomach. "Don't you have it written down somewhere?"

"I *said* I know it like my birthday."

She flicked the match over the bar counter. "Maybe with all that's happened you forgot."

"I didn't forget." Ronnie, again, tried the combination. The safe still wouldn't open. He kicked it. Banged it. Headed upstairs.

"Where're you going, Ronnie?"

Moments later, Ronnie was in his walk-in closet. Clarice right behind. He pulled out a shoe box from the top shelf, dumped it on the floor.

Clarice said, "What're you looking for?"

Ronnie, staring into the shoe box. "It's *not* here."

"*What's* not here?"

"My codebook," turning to her with teeth bared.

Clarice pointed at the shoe box. "I don't wear Dolce & Gabbana. Roberta does so don't point your finger at me. You got a problem? Speak to her. Now, *I'm* hungry. Wanna go to Aflredo's instead of Dona Luca's? Fine. You wanna meet at McDonalds? I'll think about it. Wanna play hide-and-seek? You're on your own."

The bedroom door slammed. The front door slammed. Her car door slammed.

CHAPTER TWENTY-FIVE

The following morning, Clarice was standing atop Ronnie's basement stairway with a cigarette waiting to get smoked. She wasn't getting any closer to the crazy man down below. Ronnie had spent the whole night trying to get the safe to open. She hollered, "Ronnie, you can't open your safe, you go to a locksmith. You don't blow it up." The echo fell like a thud.

Ronnie, holding a composition C4 in his hand like a Russian anarchist, hollered, "I call a locksmith, the son of a bitch will tell everyone how much money I got."

Yelling back, "Not if he's honest."

"I don't think I wanna take the chance."

"Ronnie, just out of curiosity, why do you think everyone's crooked?"

"Remember that Wall Street guy comes down from Windermere."

"What about him?"

"Tells you he's got four kids and a wife and don't say a thing."

"I didn't fuck him. I only went out with him."

"Clarice, he fucked you; then he fucked the whole country. If you can't trust your banker, you can't trust anyone."

Halfway down the stairs. Poking her head over the rail. "Ronnie, all I'm saying is why don't you call a locksmith before blowing up all of Florida?"

Hollering back, "I got a better idea. Next time you eat Italian, lay off the garlic."

Clarice blocked him at the top of the stairway. "You read the morning paper?" Shoving the front page in his face like she was serving a subpeona. "Dee Culver is all over it."

Ronnie stared at the image of Dee. Not the girl who was there the other night. Her bright eyes, happy smile, cheery as a birthday kid about to blow out the candles.

Clarice said, "She once worked at the club."

"Good for her."

Following Ronnie down the hallway. "The media is trying to make Dee's death a job-related dispute. You should read the whole article, Ronnie. Marty gives this spiel to the reporters how he's like a father to all the girls and that it breaks his heart some son of a bitch shot her. Says Dee was an angel and only a sicko would shoot her. He's talking about *you*, Ronnie. Pointing the finger away from himself and turning it on you so that you got something to hide instead of him. Some fucking lifetime friend. You get into a bit of trouble, and he turns on you. He's the one you should've killed. Not that Hank dude."

Ronnie gripped the newspaper and stared into the other photo of Dee. A lot younger. Dancer in the club.

Clarice said, "Next time talk to the reporters instead of telling them all where to go. They're making you pay for it, Ronnie. The media are shits when it comes to that. They went and turned Marty into a regular guy with a lunch pail instead of the a-hole who set you up."

Ronnie hadn't thought of that. "*Marty* set me up?"

"Geezuz, Ronnie. I sometimes wonder about you."

"You sure about this?"

"Am I *sure*? This Hank dude owed Marty something like seventy grand. Big mouth Marty wouldn't shut up about it."

"You *knew* Hank?"

"I didn't realize who he was until I saw his photo in the paper."

"Clarice, you *saw* him in the garage."

"Yeah, I saw him in the garage from upstairs where all fatsos look alike. I think Marty got the idea to tell this Hank to score at your house instead of taking down retirees in trailer parks."

"He told you that?"

"Didn't have to. This Hank needed to score big. Marty tells him how to do it. Thinks Marty's his best friend like you do."

Ronnie, staring at the old photo of Dee in her prime. Looking nothing like the woman who was there the other night. "Dee Culver hasn't worked for us in years."

"So what? She and that Hank Kosinski are every week in the parking lot buying dope from Marty, and you don't even know it. Dee's always telling everybody how she was once the big star at the club." Looking at Ronnie. Wondering who was dumb now. "You *do* get the deeper implication of all this?"

Puzzled. "What *deeper* implication?"

"Girls all over will be thinking, why work for Ronnie Harrison if one day he'll kill me if I so much as piss him off?"

Ronnie thought about that.

Clarice added, "Roberta just called. Said no one showed up at the club last night."

"The hell you mean no one showed up?"

"It was so dead Julia left saying she was going to sell peanuts on the beach."

"I'll straighten her out."

"Like she straightened *me* out?"

Ronnie said, "Why's everybody so afraid of that girl?"

"She's the only girl in the club you don't boss around. It's like you work for her."

"That's how I boss her around."

"Sure, Ronnie."

"You're telling me I'm afraid of Julia?"

"Ronnie," tired of getting nowhere with him, "you're nuts about Julia. Like she's your kid. You never once made a move on her. I think Hank was right."

"About what?"

"Roy LaHood."

Staring at Clarice. "Whaddya mean?"

"Hank wasn't the only one here that night."

"Who else was?"

Clarice lit another cigarette and blew smoke over Ronnie's face so that it hovered hazily like a ghost. "Take a guess."

Ronnie pulled out his phone like it was his gun.

"Who're ya calling now?"

"The locksmith."

In an hour, Bob the Locksmith was in front of Ronnie Harrison's basement safe with an opened canvass tool bag at his side. He turned to Ronnie. "It's not the lock."

Ronnie said, "You think it's the wrong combination?"

"No. They all open when you pass zero, maybe go down as far as ninety-five, ninety-two, but they all open. I can feel it want to. The combination is right. It's not the lock."

"So why won't it open?"

"Ask the guy who last opened it."

"I'm the guy last opened it."

"You glue this or something, Mr. Harrison?"

"Hey, I'm paying you to open this, not be funny."

"Look, problem is not the lock. I can hear it."

"Maybe you don't know about this lock. I'm not paying you; you don't have a clue."

"All locks have the same basic design, Mr. Harrison. They got three tumblers on the side, and it hasn't changed since Lincoln was breathing. You see what I'm doing?" Turning the dial and listening with a master lock stethoscope, "I'm lining up the notch of each wheel so that the fence falls into the gates of the wheels, and as long as I keep turning the dial it'll retract the bolt and open the safe. I don't care what safe it is: Fort Knox, yours. It opens. So the problem here is not the safe. It's the door. It's stuck. Now, you're absolutely sure you're the last person to open it?"

"I'm the only person *ever* opens it."

Sitting back on his heels. "Well, Mr. Harrison. You wanna torch this?"

"I just want it opened."

"Okay, but lemme ask you—"

"What?"

"You got diamonds in the safe?"

"Why do you wanna know I got diamonds in the safe?"

"Diamonds, I wouldn't worry. Cash you got a problem."

"What makes you think I got cash?"

"Don't ask me. For some reason rich people like to keep it in a safe. I don't know why."

Ronnie said, "You think I'm rich?"

"Looks it to me."

"I am not rich."

Bob said, "This your house?"

Stepping back. "Just live in it."

"That your boat outside?"

As if stepping off it. "Just use it."

"You're rich, Mr. Harrison." Bob stood up. Tool bag in hand. "Think it over," giving Ronnie his card. "We get this safe open, we'll know what's the problem."

Bob the Locksmith headed toward the basement stairway. When they reached the top step, Ronnie tapped him on the shoulder. "You got that torch with you?"

Bob pointed to the bag under his arm. They headed back down the stairs.

An hour later Ronnie headed upstairs like he was going to throw up. Clarice was in a two-piece, nibbling a Dorito. "I'm starving. Where we going?"

Ronnie pulled his white Mercedes out of the garage. Clarice came out the front door, ready for some pasta, but Ronnie was already gone.

CHAPTER TWENTY-SIX

"You shorted me four hundred dollars, Ronnie, and I'm coming down to get it."

Ronnie had something else on his mind besides Julia's paycheck. He pulled into the club parking lot. Opened the car door and felt the full force of Florida's heat rise up his legs. He grabbed Roberta's shoe box. Walked past her Beamer: name up above in the reserved slot. Then past Marty's two-tone baby-blue-and-white VW bus, the only other vehicle in town that had a surfboard on the roof because he thought it looked Sixties cool, "Surfin' USA" cool.

Ronnie put his phone in his back pocket and reached for the big aluminum flathead watering can near the bed of flowers along the cement wall. The only hint it was a gentleman's club was the Tote Him Pole planted near the curb. The scripted *T* hung a lady's golden slipper on the upward curve.

Roberta watched Ronnie make his grand entrance into the office. "Where's the fucking gardener?"

Roberta noticed her Dolce & Gabbana shoe box in his other hand.

"You fired the gardener, Ronnie."

"When?"

"I'll get one of the girls to water the flowers later."

"They're all dead."

"The *girls*?"

"The flowers."

"We'll get new ones, Ronnie."

Mimicking her: *We'll get new ones.*

Roberta, uneasy, unsure, stared at her shoe box from the wide perimeter of her granite top desk. "Maybe you wanna sit down, take a rest, Ronnie. I'll get you something to drink."

Ronnie, puzzled. "Why?"

"Past couple of days, ya know."

"You telling me how to run my business?"

Ronnie approached the big old safe that had been modeled after a French armoire. Roberta was wondering why Ronnie was opening it. She watched him spin the dial back and forth, grip the big old-fashioned brass pub handles, and heave open the heavy massive doors. He took a long gaze inside then said with the sureness of someone who had everything in control and all the time in the world, "Did I take anything out of here?"

"Gee, I wouldn't know, Ronnie," trying to get a read on him. "You're the only one who has the combination."

He showed her the empty safe in all its glory. "What's today, Roberta?"

She gulped as if she had swallowed something too big. "Thursday?"

"You asking me or telling me?"

"Ronnie—"

"If it's Thursday, Roberta, *any* Thursday, the safe shouldn't be empty."

"You asking me or telling me?"

"You being *smart*, Roberta?"

"Look, Ronnie, ever since that little shooting incident at your house, business has been slow around here. In fact, it's been completely dead with all the media blitz. People are scared to come here. I'm doing all I can to keep this place alive."

Ronnie played it cool. "Roberta, *who's* been here today?"

"The girls. It's payday."

"Who else?"

"You."

"Besides me, Roberta."

"Dumbbell Marty."

"Who else."

"The cleaning crew."

"Who else?"

"Henry the lighting guy?"

"You're getting close."

"I *am?*"

"*You're* here every day."

Looking at Ronnie. The weird smile on his face.

Ronnie pointing to the safe. "It's empty. Just as I had expected."

Roberta thinking: Roy. They both were, but differently.

Again. Calmly. "Roberta. *You* have the keys to the office."

"Yes."

"The security code to the building."

"You have a copy, too, Ronnie."

"Why would I rob myself?"

Roberta shrank back in her chair.

He showed her the safe again. "It's empty. Like the one at my house."

Roberta wanted to kill Roy.

Ronnie said, "You've lived with me the past three years and have had access to everything in my life."

"Look, Ronnie, we haven't been getting along lately. The sudden split-up, which you never explained. You throw me out of your house for no reason at all. That bitch Clarice moves in."

"What's it gotta do with my safe?"

"I'm just saying—"

"The fuck're you saying?"

"I didn't take your money, Ronnie."

"But your husband did."

"I can't find my husband. Roy walked out on me the night I brought him home. I have no idea where he is."

Turning to the wide-open empty safe. "Is this how you two operate?"

"I took *nothing*, Ronnie. I *swear*. Check the security cameras."

"You know how to turn them off."

"Doesn't mean I turned 'em off, Ronnie."

"Unless you and your husband wanted them off."

"I swear, Ronnie: I didn't rob your safe, though I wouldn't put it past Roy. He's the one you should have a talk with."

"I'm having a talk with you, Roberta," leaving the safe door open. "Buford told me that your husband and Lawton Gibbs never used a gun on a job."

"They didn't need to."

"But *you* have a gun, Roberta."

"Yes. To protect myself. I'm a woman," reaching for the drawer below her desk. Thinking she might be in need of some protection now.

"Is it loaded?"

Not sure where he was going. "Why?"

"Take it out."

"*Why?*"

"*Take* it out."

Roberta slowly opened the drawer and placed the Browning .40 caliber on her desktop.

"Point it at me."

"Why, Ronnie?"

"If you can point it at me, you can point it at anybody."

"I don't understand."

"I don't give a fuck. Point it at me."

Roberta picked up the Browning and cautiously aimed it at him. Her shooting finger just outside the trigger guard.

Ronnie walked over to the safe and opened it again. "Now, if Roy, your husband, walks in here right now and tries to rob the safe, what do you do?"

"I'd have a talk with him."

"I didn't say Donald Duck, Roberta. I said, *Roy*."

"Ronnie, he'd have to walk in here for me to find out."

"Okay. He just did. *I'm* Roy, and I, Roy LaHood, am in the process of stealing all the club's money."

Roberta, playing along. "I'm calling the police, Roy."

"I'll be gone by the time they get here."

"How do you know?"

Ronnie began to lose patience. "The reason you bought that gun, Roberta, was some guy comes in here tries to rob, rape, or abuse you again, you stand your ground."

"But Roy's not committing a crime against me. So I just can't shoot him."

"He's committing a crime against the club, and *you* work for the club."

"Geezuz, Ronnie, I'm not a lawyer."

"You don't have to be. When you're in a situation that's real, you don't think about the law; you think about your ass. So I want you to think about your ass, Roberta."

"I'm really trying, Ronnie."

"Give it *another* try."

Still not sure where he was going, but guessing long. "You want me to kill you, Ronnie? I mean—are you depressed or something?"

"No. I want you to kill, *Roy*."

"But," looking around, "Roy's *not* here."

"Make believe I'm Roy."

Playing along. Aiming the forty caliber at him. "I'm not gonna press the trigger, Ronnie."

"Why?"

"Because then it's not make-believe."

"Okay, we'll make it real." The raw injury of betrayal was bare as Ronnie took the cover off the Dolce & Gabbana shoe box and removed his Glock and fired. Roberta's eyes were so vacant they looked like they'd been robbed.

CHAPTER TWENTY-SEVEN

Marty was behind the bar, stamping bags of coke with his orange basketball logo, when he thought he heard something go off all the way down by the office. He could've checked out the disturbance, but leaving a pound of coke around wasn't cool. So he finished stamping. Hid the bags in a slot under the bar next to his sawed-off shotgun. Poured another three lines. Rolled up a twenty and snorted deeply. The show floor was empty and quiet. All the table chairs had been leaned over. It was the time of day a mouse could get very unlucky if a cat were around. Marty was about to do the third line of coke when he saw something strange flare up in the big bar mirror. It was hollow and incomplete. Its gaze pitched forward as it coalesced into a person or part of one. Marty, one eyeball on the line of coke, the other on the floating figure, was beginning to feel that this was more than a momentary intrusion into his private party. He dropped the funneled bill on the counter, thinking maybe he should stop doing coke this early in the afternoon. Maybe shoot some hoops. Jog on the beach. Get back in shape. Call that divorced woman down the street he'd been trying to seduce while his wife was out trying to sell real estate to people who couldn't get mortgages. But what he really needed was good sex. The kind that satisfied for days. The kind his wife couldn't give him because she was too busy whining about everyone trying to screw her out of a commission. He snorted up the last line of coke then cleaned off the counter. Tossed the rag in the bar sink. Washed his hands and spread on a little cream. He looked up to make sure that whatever had been in the mirror had never really been there. But it was now closer and following him as he tried to back away. It made a flat wheezing hum that was barely audible, as if having moved from some other dimension to this one had compressed everything into a streaming hiss so it could sing "Fly Me to the Moon." Then the apparition disappeared. The room was empty. Except for Ronnie who was standing at the far end of the main floor. He staggered across and pushed a barstool under his butt. "Pour me a Grey Goose straight up with a lemon twist."

Marty thought Ronnie looked weird. His bloodshot eyes heavy in his skull.

"You gonna make me that drink?"

"Sure, Ronnie. You hear anything before?"

"Like what?"

"A truck backfiring." Marty made Ronnie his Goose and set it on the bar top with a napkin and a stirrer.

Ronnie saw the trace of coke on the bar top. "*Stoned* again?"

Marty, eyes supercharged, gave the remaining line a swipe. "Nah, just dust."

"Bullshit."

"I'm telling you the truth, Ronnie."

"And I suppose the only reason LeBron plays for the Cavaliers is that you don't like Cleveland in the winter."

Marty spoke as a concerned friend. "You feeling okay, Ronnie?" Wondering what was going on.

"Sure. *You* feeling okay? Pour me another."

Marty poured. "Pretty big thing you did the other night," making a gun with his thumb and forefinger. "I guess those two bums took you for an easy mark," not getting a laugh. "You want something to feel better?" Making a face, as if to say: *I won't tell.*

Ronnie said, "You remember a girl named Dee?"

"Who?"

"Dee Culver. Worked here. Friend of yours."

"Lotta girls come in here looking for something, Ronnie. That's our business."

"I'm talking about Dee the junkie. Used to work the pole. Tall, thin, large-breasted girl. Looked like a voodoo doll, Amy Winehouse, all that mascara. You used to call her 'Hot Pants' because you thought she liked it."

"I still don't remember."

Ronnie tried again. "She sang while she danced. Couldn't carry a tune and made everyone laugh."

"What about it?"

"You ever hit on her?"

"Probably. Who remembers? I fuck a lot of girls."

"Sure ya do, Marty. How long ago did she work here?"

"You'll have to check your books. I'm not the bookkeeper."

"I don't have to check shit. I checked with Clarice. Funny how with someone's help your memory all of a sudden comes back. It turns out Dee's been your customer for years. Then she had to leave the club because she was too stoned to find the dance pole, but you continued selling to her anyway. Tell me, Marty. When did she first get short and couldn't pay you?"

"I have no idea what you're talking about, Ronnie," busy drying a glass that was dry.

"I'll ask you again."

"I still don't know what you're talking about."

"You sold junk to that biker, Hank Kosinski, on a percentage condition with interest; you figuring the guy was somewhere on the level and you could double your money."

"I don't sell drugs, Ronnie."

"You *don't* sell drugs? Tell that to the police."

"The police?"

"They get all worked up about stuff like that."

"Look, Ronnie," tapping his fingers on the bar top, "what I do is do people favors. Everybody wants a favor around here, so I try and help out. Grease the wheels. Help business. Help *you*, Ronnie. But I'm not a drug dealer."

"Marty, when you give drugs to someone, they give you money?"

"We make an *exchange* is the closest word I can think."

"I presume someone has to pay you, or you won't give them blow, right?"

Marty's eyes drifted. "I'm not too sure what you mean."

"You give it to them for nothing?"

"Ronnie, I like to give. Xmas I give to the poor."

"*Not* blow. There's a difference."

"There is?" Marty made a face like he was stuck with an idiot.

Ronnie said, "And that difference is what's known as an agreed compact that's reciprocated versus something that just casually happens between people."

Marty, tired of getting lectured. "Everybody's my friend, Ronnie. I like to help people."

"Sure you do, Marty, and when someone gives you money, they're in effect paying you for a service rendered. Tell me I'm wrong."

"I give 'em stuff, Ronnie. If they leave money on the table, what am I supposed to do? Throw it out?"

"Not unless the money was to pay off a debt, which is what an exchange is."

"Ronnie. I do people favors. I don't make it complicated."

"Then I'll do *you* a favor. One that's *not* complicated. Dee Culver and Hank Kosinski couldn't pay you. So you tell them you know somebody up in Sailfish Point has a lot of money. Maybe they can find something up there to pay you what they owe you."

"Ronnie, what you say offends me."

"Marty—"

"What?"

"Remember those Goldman Sachs guys."

"Not really."

"Ones that testified before Congress concerning the 'Shitty Deal.'"

"What shitty deal?"

"The 'Goldman Sachs Wall Street Shitty Deal.' It was all over the news after the economy tanked back in '08. There were congressional hearings for days, weeks."

"Never heard of it, Ronnie."

"Then I'll refresh your memory. Goldman Sachs sells a security, what they call a 'synthetic collateralized debt obligation,' worth a zillion dollars that's really worthless shit and doesn't tell its investors, despite the fact Goldman Sachs is being paid to give these same investors financial advice. The reason is that Goldman Sachs is planning on shorting the whole fucking deal. This guy Michael Swenson, head mortgage trader at Goldman, says, and I quote, 'Cause maximum pain.' Have these suckers 'totally demoralized.' In fact, people on the other end of the deal, like John Paulson, the hedge-fund manager, were shorting it along with Goldman. He was allowed to pick and choose the collateral that the unwitting original investors had bought, and when the collateral tanked, Goldman Sachs and friends raked in a combined two billion dollars from the short. Not bad for an economy that just flushed over ten trillion dollars of bad mortgage loans down the toilet and put millions worldwide in the shithole."

"Why should that concern me, Ronnie?"

"Because Marty, sending Dee Culver and Hank Kosinski over to my house was a *shitty deal.*"

Marty took a rag and started wiping down the already wiped-down bar. Ronnie put his hand in the way. "What's that song Dee used to sing when she danced? She'd sing it real slowly. Look up at the ceiling and spread her arms out like a bird."

Marty looked up. Then it all came back. "You mean 'Fly Me to the Moon'?"

"Yeah, Marty. That's the song. I need your shotgun."

"Huh?"

"One you hide under the bar in case of a holdup."

"For what?"

"For a few hours."

"Why?"

"I'm your boss. *That's* why."

Marty didn't like the look in Ronnie's eyes. No different than his first wife's when it'd become evident that her trust in him had been replaced with a seething hatred and a desire to kill him. Marty reached under the bar and pulled out the sawed-off. Ronnie shot first. Marty fell back into the second row of bottles. Blood rushed out of his nose as if he had just sneezed. The expression on his face hollow as the hollow point that jammed his skull. Then a stream of sunlight poured into the clubroom as a golden figure appeared in the doorway. Ronnie said, as if he were the next-door neighbor picking up the morning paper, "How did your college interview go?"

Julia, looking for the sound she had heard. "I want my *four* hundred dollars."

"What four hundred?"

"The money you took out of my salary for that topless stunt."

Ronnie counted four bills and stretched out his hand. "You know I like to have a little fun."

Julia felt something wet under her foot.

Ronnie looked down. "Something happened."

She followed the blood to the bar. "You stood your ground again?"

"Yeah."

"Well look who's standing in it now."

CHAPTER TWENTY-EIGHT

Roy was enjoying life for the first time in years. He had money and a crazy girl named Wanda who was more than a handful. She liked to be tied at the wrists, but not too tightly. Playfully spanked, but not too hard. Most of all she loved role-playing: a central component to her art and her lifestyle. She turned Roy into a vice cop from a small Southern town with a single jail then into a preacher with a gimp who hated smut and loose girls more than he loved Jesus.

Roy said, "Anybody else you want me to be?"

"Yeah," slipping on a skirt, pointing to the wall.

They crammed themselves into the closet and made believe they were in a Jumbo Jet cruising at forty thousand feet. Wanda was Fancy Nancy the Stewardess and Roy was Mr. Harold Fischberger, a pharmaceutical salesman from Toledo: bald and farsighted with oversized glasses. Mr. Fischberger got locked in the restroom. Fancy Nancy knocked on the door. Harold opened it and dragged her inside.

When Wanda got tired of the closet gig, she became an actress in a producer's office with a casting couch. She bawled out the producer, a Mr. Roy Finkel, for being an unethical, nonprogressive, antifeminist jerk for trying to seduce her, and in the process she, to her complete surprise, was thrown over his knees and thoroughly spanked, and *only* then, after some tearful contrition, could she audition for the upcoming role of Honey in *Who's Afraid of Virginia Wolf?* stark naked while doing jumping jacks with her tongue sticking out.

Roy thought this chick was weird. Especially when she wanted to play waitress and get caught stealing from the till. Wanda insisted that there had to be real money in the make-believe cash register; otherwise, it wouldn't have the same effect on her libido.

Wanda said, "Just put a whole bunch of money in the top drawer, like ten thousand dollars, and I'll skip over there and take it, and you catch me."

Roy said, "I ain't got that kinda money."

Wanda turned her nose up. "Oh, yes you do." Pointing under the bed. "I found some in a big sack while I was cleaning out all that dust this morning."

Roy wasn't role-playing when he said, "Who the fuck told you to clean up?"

Wanda wasn't going to answer a silly question like that. Impatient for the fun to begin, she said, "Roy, if you don't get the money, I will." She got down on the floor and met Roy's eyes at the other end of the bed—there wasn't a thing between them. Roy said, "Where'd ya put it, Wanda?"

"Put what?"

"What was under here."

Playing insulted to the hilt, Wanda got up from the floor. So did Roy, thinking: *Some housecleaner.* Getting into it, Wanda said, "I'm sorry sir, but I didn't overcharge you." Her nose up in the air.

"I'll ask you again. Where'd ya put the goddamn duffel bag?"

"I refuse to even answer such a silly question. I'm as honest as the day is long," really into it now.

Roy, standing over her. "You don't tell me where you put the duffel bag, your ass is *really* gonna get spanked."

"Roy, that's not the tone of voice I like to use in role-play."

"I'll use whatever tone of voice I want."

Wanda pouted, "I don't wanna play anymore," but they were already off script.

Audrey caught sight of Wanda and Roy running toward the beach from the bungalow. Wanda in her waitress outfit. Roy stark naked with oversized glasses. He chased Wanda back into the bungalow. Wanda went out the front door, Roy right behind. The neighbors on the lawn made some choice comments, including a dog who joined in the chase. Audrey, not interested in local shenanigans, took her phone out of her beach bag and called Julia. She needed the Monster for the afternoon lessons down at the pool. She was thinking maybe Julia was late because the professor was giving her a tour of the campus. Showing her the labs where Julia would be doing premed. Introducing her to the faculty. Talking about the courses she'd be taking in the fall, all the clubs, sororities, the nice kids and good things for once in her life. Audrey folded her lounge chair and headed home. Maybe Julia was already back. Her phone turned off because she didn't want to be bothered. Audrey went through the rear door and was about to put her beach bag down when she saw Lawton sitting at the kitchen table looking like a bank teller on payday with piles of cash condominium high.

He said, "This is what I owe y'all for the years I been gone."

Audrey approached the table as if it were radioactive. "Where did you get all this money?"

"It's lost and found."

"You did this alone or with Roy?"

"We thought there'd be a lot more, but who's complaining?"

"They'll catch you, Lawton. Send you back to prison."

"I did it for you and Julia knowing going back to prison would be a possibility, but also knowing I took care of my family. I owe it to all y'all. It's been bothering me for ten years."

"All that money could be marked."

"Won't matter. I'm taking it to an offshore bank where you and Julia will have access to it whenever y'all need it."

"How're ya gonna get it offshore, Lawton?"

"A boat."

"You bought a boat?"

"Something close to it." Lawton put the last of the money back into the duffel bag and zipped it up. He shoved it on the floor beside his chair. "I'll send you the bank information once everything is set up."

There was a knock on the door. Audrey let Roy in. He looked funny. Shirt buttons in the wrong holes. Barefoot and out of breath. Big glasses on his face.

Audrey said to him, "Since when do you wear eyeglasses?"

Roy threw them in the garbage. "Mind if I sit down?"

"You're hungry again?"

"No. Somebody stole my duffel bag."

Lawton said, "Well, this one here is from the club."

"I ain't accusing you, Lawton."

Lawton said, "You leave your bungalow today?"

"Only this morning for a swim with Wanda and I know I locked all the doors 'cause I triple-checked."

"How about the windows?"

"Shut like a tomb." Roy turned to the front door.

Julia entered. She tossed the Ducati keys on the kitchen table and noticed the duffel bag. "Somebody going camping?" She took the fourth seat, next to her mother, and put her arm around her.

Audrey said, "How did the interview go?"

"So-so. What do *they* want?"

Roy said to Julia, "Where was Crystal last night?"

"You got bigger problems than that."

"I waited all day for her."

"You didn't hear what I said, Roy."

"Where the hell is she?"

"I don't have a clue."

"Has she been back to the bungalow?"

"Why?"

"Because she got the keys to it."

"Good for her."

"Maybe bad for her."

"I don't think you understand."

"Girl, I don't think *you* understand."

Julia took out her phone, tapped the app, and showed Roy a photo of Roberta slumped on the floor.

"This some kinda joke?"

"You see me laughing?"

"What happened?"

"Well, it all depends on whose story you want to believe," looking at Roy, her father, and then the duffel bag at his side. "Ronnie thinks you and Roberta robbed his safe at the club and at his home. Said he tried to get the truth out of Roberta at the office, but she pulled a gun on him because she knew the gig was up. I guess she forgot to unlock it. That was the first thing the police noticed when they took it out of her hand."

Roy said, "You saw all this?"

"I got there after it happened. Ronnie called the police. Went on down to the station and told them the whole story. How it was all connected to the robbery at his house."

"Well Ronnie ain't the only one been robbed."

Julia looked down at the duffel bag and then at Roy. "Roberta and Marty Bannister are dead. Who's next?"

"I didn't kill anyone." Missing the point.

CHAPTER TWENTY-NINE

It took Ronnie forever to get home. Twice he turned onto I-95 to drive all the way up to Bayonne to visit his cousin Val. She said, "Come on up, Ronnie, before someone else tries and kills you." Twice he turned back.

Ronnie could've been at Val's ranch house in two days if he stepped on it. He'd be drinking beer, eating barbecue, dipping pickles, flushing hands in bowls of popcorn. He'd get so drunk the house, the trees, the leaves, and the sky would look like bubbles and balloons—then what?

As soon as he entered the mansion, Clarice was on his case about a dinner party at the tennis club that evening. She wasn't going to be late like she was to everything else in his life. Ronnie hid in the bathroom. Half hour later he blew out in a towel. Clarice aimed her nail file at him. "If you're late one more time, I'm through with you, Ronnie."

Ronnie disappeared into his walk-in closet. Clarice followed. He said, "Where're we eating tonight?" Coming out with a tennis outfit because now he remembered.

"I told you, Ronnie. Everybody's gotta wear white. But if we never get there, who cares?"

"Why white?"

"Geezuz, Ronnie, it's theme night. Chris Evert's gonna be there."

"So what?"

"Ronnie, the whole club is wearing in white."

"Why white all of a sudden?"

"Because back in the day they wore all-white outfits, white frilly tennis panties and played with real wooden rackets and white balls. Girls looked great a hundred years ago."

"*Fifty* years ago."

"What's the difference?"

"Fuck, theme night. I'll wear what I want."

Clarice turned on the TV while Ronnie put on his outfit: a color-blast tennis T-shirt, purple shorts, and a pair of neon-green Gel Resolution court shoes. Clarice yelled, "*Hey, Ronnie,* get your ass over here!"

A hotshot TV reporter was reliving the last moments of Roberta and Marty as she imagined it to have happened at close range. Getting a chair. Rolling off the chair. Eyes wide open. Ronnie grabbed the remote and turned the power off.

Clarice hollered, "The hell happened today?"

"Roberta got cute in the office and pulled a gun on me when I opened my safe."

"The hell for?"

"There was *nothing* in it."

"They robbed that too?"

"Yeah and on my way out dumbbell Marty grabs the sawed-off he keeps under the bar and tries to off me. But the cops they were very understanding."

"You called them?"

"Yeah, I called them. Showed them the empty safe. Everything just the way it happened. Roberta's gun in her hand. The pound of cocaine Marty hid under the bar. I said go ahead and arrest me. Check and see if my fingerprints are on her gun, like I set it up or something. I will fully cooperate. Buford met me at the station. Everybody was cool. No yelling or shouting. Some paperwork and handshaking. There's nothing to worry about. All I gotta do is show up in court and answer a few questions."

Clarice slipped on her white tennis skirt. "Well, I hope you had some topless girls down at the police station."

Ronnie looked up from tying his tennis shoes. "The hell for?"

"Otherwise, you're gonna have to pay Buford."

Ronnie headed out the bedroom.

"*Sometimes* you have no sense of humor, Ronnie."

CHAPTER THIRTY

The following morning a servant placed a soft-boiled egg in Mrs. Johnson's eggcup and the one across from her. Mrs. Johnson said, "Tell Mr. Gibbs that his breakfast is getting cold." The servant immediately left.

Mrs. Johnson, alone at the table, stared out into the Atlantic Ocean and watched the morning sun rise from its celestial pit. She was thinking of Egypt. The oppressing heat in the Valley of the Kings. Karnak: its massive temple columns hosting Germans in their hiking bloomers. Italians in their gladiator sandals. Swedes in their disposable paper underwear. Irish green with envy. The horse in her father's Charleston stall named Nefertiti. Her first kiss in the garden next to it. The coloreds tending flowers. The dogs barking as the boys left. The Southern sun turning red as the rain passed through a world that seemed to have been created five minutes ago with a given past memory. How odd to suddenly be old. Time nothing but a wink. A trick aimed at those busy born and dying.

Lawton entered the breakfast room. He quietly pulled out his chair. Looked down at his egg. The two strips of bacon. The white toast. Jam dish. Butter dish. Salt shaker. Orange juice. Black coffee. Napkin. Milk. Then at the woman across the table from him who somehow looked double the size and double the trouble. "I just spoke to Julia."

"And?"

"She didn't say no."

Mrs. Johnson put a teaspoon to her egg and cracked the shell. "Good. I shall stop by after breakfast." She finished her egg. Walked out the room. Rang the chauffeur. Left the house.

The black Bentley Mulsanne ignored the Surfside parking rules and drove on past the cluster of bungalows. A woman, with big Jackie O sunglasses, poked her head out of the rear window. From afar, the sedan looked like a spaceship had landed and a bug-eyed creature was making a test of the atmosphere. Mrs. Johnson exited the Bentley and landed in a world bordering on insolvency. Gertie's junk was still outside Herb's bungalow. The one across the way was neater, but as with any home short of space, everything spilled out. Surfboards of various sizes and uses were stacked up against the wall. Bicycles had fallen over. Handlebars were turned back like the heads of roped calves. A boogie board, wash line, barbecue grill, and a scruffy black Italian motorcycle shared the small yard with a standup Craftsman toolbox. Metric wrenches were spread out on the grass. Motor oil and strong coffee weighed heavily in the air. A gray metal locker had been set up against the side wall and was filled, top to bottom, with leather racing suits, helmets, track boots, bikinis, skydiving gear, flippers, goggles, and a blackjack: Flatbush issue. So small was the space that it created its own interior maze of lost and forgotten things. Mrs. Johnson, overwhelmed, proceeded to the front door and stumbled over a power drill and nearly fell over. Angrily, she picked it up with the intention of tossing it in the garbage when she noticed a warning printed in indelible ink: *This tool belongs to Julia Gibbs. You're touching something that ain't yours.* The unexpected introduction left Mrs. Johnson with a less-than-reassuring feeling. She cautiously knocked on the front door of the white bungalow several times. Her chauffeur, standing at his post, opined, "That could be Miss Julia out on the water."

Mrs. Johnson turned past the communal ground that faced the ocean and noticed a blond-haired girl on a surfboard riding through the crest of a large wave. She rode the bull hard to shore. Then left the ocean as if stepping out of the shower. Mrs. Johnson, a horsewoman, greatly admired the girl's skill, agility, and determination. She had a defiance that seemed to extinguish any notion of fear. The adaptability good athletes and seasoned risk takers maximize when confronted with difficult or dangerous choices. Plus she was beautiful on a scale that tipped any other including the rigged ones that always have a finger on it.

Mrs. Johnson followed the path to the beach past several middle-aged women sitting on cheap folding lounge chairs who were more than curious at the rich lady's bling, as if the beach had put in a request to be accessorized. Mrs. Johnson turned back to the Bentley. The uniformed chauffeur, with experienced fingers, tipped the passenger door closed. Then she said to the passing comet, "Are you Julia Gibbs?"

Julia looked up at the tall woman whose face hung in the sky like the moon. Her demeanor imcompatible against the spectacle of beachballs, flipflops, and bagged lunches.

"I should like to have a word with you if you are."

Julia poked a finger at the antique. "You're here for a surfing lesson?"

"Most certainly not."

"Well you're head of the line if ya want one."

"I'm not here for surfing lessons, young lady."

Julia spotted the big shiny black sedan up the road with the man dressed in livery standing at his post like a carved indian.

Mrs. Johnson said, "I feel it a courtesy as much as an obligation to introduce myself as the woman who will shortly be your stepmother."

Julia, surfboard in tow, took in the tall and lean courtly woman infused with the tony glint of too many couture shows and gallery openings of art so narrow and thin of its own disorder that it reeked of aesthetic inbreeding. Julia was thinking there must be some latent hormone that surfaces after a certain age that makes fashionable rich old gals draft wild color-clashing fabrics like soldiers in time of war and festoon themselves with whimsical sashes, hot patterned pantaloons, oversized eyeglass frames of Muse Funk yellow or pink or red or white, whacky toe paint, animated jewelry, plastic beaded jack-in-the-box hats, geisha socks, death-proof lipstick, bubble-bath hair, and oversized bangs, but then Julia didn't know what it was like to have lost the scorching rawness of youth and still feel young at heart, a secret no woman of years reveals without the risk of some background snickering: the penalty for trying to engage eyes no longer interested. Julia turned to the black sedan thick with its own layers of paint, primers, and industrial gloss: "Who's the bozo by the car?"

"My chauffeur and he's *not* a bozo."

"Tell him I don't need a stepmother. Tell him I got a mother who'll do just fine. Tell him to take the old lady he brought back home. Tell him the next time she asks him to do something dumb to quit his job and come work for me. I need a good man around the bungalow."

"Why don't you tell him yourself?"

"It's more fun telling you."

"You may think you're cute, young lady, but I don't. I'm going to be your stepmother and you better get used to the idea."

"Stepmother my ass."

Mrs. Johnson swung at Julia, but swiftness was wanting. She landed flat on her back, blacked out into some other dimension where her hair was 1950s short. Her father's Piedmonts and Deuces Wild in her purse. Then onto Istanbul, where she lay half naked in a hotel room after having been raped as the staff fetched her down the elevator like a cow. The smell of pungent sweat and market dung still in her nose. It trailed her when she flew off the tarmac in a wobbly prop back to Rome and was with her when she pulled into Oslo. Then back to London. Her father just in from Paris as they dined at the Naval Club; and still the septic sweat, the discolored teeth, the weighted grunts, the pillow over her face, and that Istanbul hotelier dressed in heavy wool and tarboosh telling her that it had been a poor man who had perpetrated the crime, suggesting a burden of guilt on her part. Fearful she wouldn't pay the bill, the Turk hauled her out of her room, called the police, and threatened her with jail where guards walked over grates and poured down the daily slop.

Back in London, the IV Leaguers danced with her at all the clubs and then onto a strip joint where an English sailor with a chipped tooth and a Welsh grin, as freckled as a rainbow trout, put his arms around her and breathed brown beer into her tipsy lips while she closed her eyes and woke up the next morning surrounded by a dozen empty bottles of Double Diamond. She asked the sailor if he had a gun. He laughed as he shaved off her smell. She called her father. But he was gone. A note had been left with the concierge: *Business in Stuttgart. See you in Charleston.* He meant the French Quarter. South of Broad. Her brand-new Chevy Bel Air Blue Flame waiting in the carriage house. The memory of Istanbul parked beside it as Mrs. Johnson, now back in this dimension, squinted in the Florida sun with eyes as wet and as damp as the surf breaching the shoreline.

Julia said, as she helped the elderly woman up, "You all right?"

Mrs. Johnson reached for something that wasn't there. "My pocketbook."

"Here." Julia checked to see if anything had fallen out. "Maybe you should sit down."

"*No.*" Mrs. Johnson brushed the sand off and planted her feet squarely on terra firma with more than a bit of shame. "I suppose the need to make a connection can sometimes be so terribly awkward that it is plainly embarrassing."

"Your left hook showed it," Julia said.

Mrs. Johnson held onto her for support. "That's not what I mean, young lady. I'm talking about how I met your father. How it all came to this. You need to hear me, because there are rumors and lies that have been egregiously spread."

"I couldn't care less."

"I do. Your father came out of nowhere to rob me blind."

"He usually comes out of nowhere."

"Then he talked to me."

"You oughta wear flats, not heels."

"He took the pills out of my hand and saved my life."

"Your chauffeur is waving at us."

Mrs. Johnson waved him off. "Your father said that you do not face death in war in as much as you face your fears, and I had more than enough of my own. My failed political ambitions. My access to power with a man who had kept all that power to himself and who chose his mistresses and weekends like his shirts and ties."

"Why did you betray my father if he risked his life to save yours?"

"It was my husband who sent him to jail. He returned home from a business trip and got his lawyers and all his men. Fearful that I might lose everything, I did whatever they wanted, which was to turn Lawton in. You see, Leyland had been my lifeline all those years. I dared not contradict nor confront him, but when he died, all that was his became mine. I reached for my pen. At first hesitantly. Then guiltily. Then rashly. Then boldly and uncompromisingly. Your father and I reestablished our friendship, not easily, but progressively. I asked him for forgiveness, and like the Southern gentleman he is, he gave it."

"I don't believe you."

"You can believe what you want, but I'm here to make a connection that will last more than a few days. Let us start out not as enemies, but as friends. I want nothing of you other than the decency and kindness that you would expect of another person."

"Look, this whole thing about my father is not about love, and you know it."

"Maybe, but at my age it's about something more important."

"What?"

"Companionship. And with that, I want to help you get ahead in this world." Mrs. Johnson picked a flower and handed it to Julia. "Your father says you're an expert rider. You can jump a five-foot fence."

"So what?"

"You're an expert skydiver."

"What about it?"

"He said you're one in a million."

"No, he didn't."

"He did say that he loved you very much."

They reached the big lawn where people gathered to sit in the sun by age, interest, and wit. Mrs. Johnson said, "Please give me a chance. That's all I'm asking." The flower, now on the grass.

Julia stared at the big, shiny sedan. Its shell glazed like a doughnut. "Tell ya what. Let me drive that car of yours, and I'll see what I can do."

Mrs. Johnson, not sure about the girl's driving experience, warned, "As long as we get home in one piece."

Julia took the keys from the chauffeur. "You forget. I'm *already* home."

CHAPTER THIRTY-ONE

Several old leather photo albums of black album paper were spread open on a desk in Mrs. Johnson's study. Julia pointed to the dull script underneath an old black-and-white Brownie shot faded at the corners. It was overexposed and printed flat. The sky nothing more than a paper backdrop to the colonial building that housed the classrooms.

"What's Radcliffe?"

Mrs. Johnson said, "That's where I went to college."

"I thought you went to Harvard."

"In those days Harvard was just for men. Radcliffe was its sister college."

Julia said, "What did you major in?"

"Political science."

"Why?"

"Why not?" She turned a page. "Here I am at twenty-five. I was in New York with my father on business, and he was introducing me to people in the fashion industry. I told him I wanted to sit in on his meetings. Discuss strategy, markets, and how we could use psychology to better understand the buying habits of our customers and how to use emotion, not reason, to gain their loyalty. I had no desire to prance about on a runway or do silly things that required no imagination or hard thinking. I wanted to build something. Be part of something. Not represent something."

"Your father was in the fashion business?"

"He was on the board of several major corporations and pulled many strings. That's what I wanted to do." Pointing to another photo. "You see, I was exceptionally intelligent with a gift for insight and quick analysis; smarter and sharper than all the dull men I knew and they resented it. So, you can understand how I found it distressing and frustrating to be ignored. The game was so very rigid back then. I don't think you really understand how difficult it was, Julia. The world, back in the Fifties, was rigidly defined by gender, race, and religion, and in spite of the progress we've made, those regressive agents who were against us then are still against us now as they shift their resentment, fear, and hatred to newer targets."

"Well, no one is stopping me."

"And that's what I like about you, Julia. You have an indomitable spirit. I may be years older than you, but deep at heart we were destined to have met. Destined to help each other for some greater purpose unknown to us."

They headed down the hall that was more like a gangplank where the sightline was above and below.

Julia said, "I like the room where everything slides open into shelves and the water in the shower pours down on you from all sides. I like all of that, but I wouldn't trade it for where I live."

Not believing Julia. "Would you like that room?"

"Would I *like* it?"

"It could be yours if you want."

"I got my own room in my own bungalow and I'm my own boss."

"Of course, but the room here could be yours as well. You'll have access to the house anytime you want. You'll be a member of the family. You may ride my horses down at the stable. Bring your friends over for a swim. Use the three-hole golf course I have out back. Your father said you swing a club perfectly from the inside."

"Yeah, well, *he* doesn't. He chicken wings it, unless he improved since prison."

Mrs. Johnson took Julia by the hand and led her to a wide-open room that faced the Atlantic Ocean. "This is my special place. Come."

Julia sat in a lounge chair that was a long piece of curved black leather that hugged her body at $195 per inch. Her flip-flops dangled over as the chaise automatically tilted back and made her feel as if she were floating miles above Earth. Mrs. Johnson took a framed photo off the wall and showed it to her. "Ellen was my one and only child." She rested it on her lap. "I come here and stare at her for hours. This was taken in Gramercy Park, New York City, many years ago. I want to believe Ellen's alive somewhere, even though I know she isn't. Both of us suffered the same fate. I survived, only to see it happen to her in a more devastating way."

Julia couldn't share in the woman's pain on such short notice, but in consolation said, "I'll take you up on that offer."

Mrs. Johnson happily rose from her chair and took Julia's hand gently and lovingly.

Julia warned, "But only under one condition."

"I can accept almost any."

"It must have nothing to do with you marrying my father."

"I want you to be my friend, Julia, whether or not I marry him."

"Good, because I've got news for you. He's still madly in love with my mother. But then you already know he doesn't love you one bit. He's just using you."

Mrs. Johnson felt the knife.

"Don't worry. He's all yours," Julia said. "My mother won't have him back."

"Why?"

"My father took a vow."

"What vow?"

"The one you take when you get married: till death do us part. And now everyone thinks my mother is too hard on him."

"Maybe she is."

"Wrong. A vow is supposed to be hard, and if you break it, it should break you."

Lying to Julia, "I wouldn't have it any other way." Realizing that loneliness, the way it shuts you out of the world, had allowed her to so foolishly imagine that she could love this younger man, gentle in manner, simple and undemanding, easy to please and always polite; yet, certainly not of her class in education, ambition, and those eclectic sensitivities that only money can cultivate and dispense before and after supper. "Did he say that he was *using* me?"

Julia said, "You're like eighty. He's forty-five. You're a zillionaire. He's broke. Need I say more?"

"Yes, but your father and I spent many hours talking. He gave me advice and strength no one else could. I'm so much stronger because of him."

"*You* are," Julia said, "but *he* isn't. I mean, what did *you* give him? *Ten* years in prison? Your jewels were the price you had to pay to learn to live, but you wanted it all."

"That's unfair, Julia. You know very well it's against the law to steal."

"I wish you people knew that. I read about your late husband online and all the predatory people he was in bed with on Wall Street that led to the crash of '08. Y'all are the ones should've been thrown in prison after selling all those unwitting investors zillions of dollars of worthless mortgages."

"We all make mistakes, Julia."

"Screwing people is *not* a mistake."

"Then you know little of the world you speak. Life is a brutal game. Unfair. Often very short and painful. But friendships are made to sidestep those enduring cruelties, and in that regard you have not only failed me, but hurt me."

"Hurt *you*? *You* hurt my mother and me. But then you're too self-absorbed to feel anyone's pain other than your own; that's *your* failure."

Mrs. Johnson reached for Julia's hand.

Julia stepped away. "What do you *really* want, Mrs. Johnson?"

"To be your friend."

"*Why*?"

"So that the cruelty of life can be mitigated by a shared love and concern."

"Well, if you want to be my friend, you better understand that I can't be bought."

"Yes, of course, Julia, but if we could just do something. Something we could both share. Something we could call our very special own. Something besides indulging in the madness of hate and revenge or it's your fault, it's her fault, but *never* my fault. You see—it's not your father I want, but *you*."

"You want *me*?"

"Yes. A frienship clean and right from the start. I will be fair, loving, honest. There for you when you need me and you there for me. It could be so beautiful rather than this empty, pointless, depressing existence of mistrust,suspcision, and constant betrayal. We can do it. I *know* we can. You and I, Julia. You and I." Feeling stronger, resolve once again fluid in her vintage veins. Love filling her heart. "I was thinking that we—"

"*What*?"

"We could skydive together."

"You want to *skydive?*" Imagining the old lady in goggles plummeting toward the earth at multiple G-forces. Julia headed out of the room. "It would kill you, ma'am."

"*Where* are you going?"

"I got things to do. Friends to meet. Surfing lessons to teach."

Mrs. Johnson, seeing her plans suddenly dissolve, straggled behind. "But, Julia," the desperateness in her voice, clear.

"Gotta go."

Mrs. Johnson clutched the bannister and leaned as far over as she could. "*Don't* you like me?"

Clemens held the front door open as Julia flew outside and hopped into the waiting Bentley. Her feet up on the closed window. Phone in hand as the big shiny sedan took off with Mrs. Johnson's question still unanswered.

CHAPTER THIRTY-TWO

Jensen Beach. The sun above and the beach below spilled out into a big scrawl. Wanda was comfortably set up in a cheap folding lounge chair, reading Roy's memoir on her iPad. She nudged him with her foot. "One moment you're in Iraq, the next you're giving cha-cha lessons at the Fontainebleau. How did you get into cat burgling?"

"By accident." Roy had his eye on two homicide detectives approaching Audrey's bungalow.

Wanda turned a page. "Were you still in the army?"

"No."

"What were you doing?"

"Hustling poolside products."

"What kind in particular, Roy?"

"The kind that folks want around the pool."

"Who was the woman who owned the company?"

"Very nice lady. Still friends with her."

"How did you get the job?"

Roy turned away from Audrey's bungalow. "What time did you clean the bungalow this morning?"

"I told you a hundred times, Roy. I just swept up because of my allergies. I *don't* clean. Other people do that for me. And you should keep your money in a bank, not under a mattress."

Audrey opened the door. The cops gave their spiel.

Wanda said, "Do you know that you can write?"

"Huh?"

"You can *write*, Roy. You write very well."

"Lot good it's done me."

"You say the owner hired Lawton because of his looks. What about you?"

"*Hey*, I'm even better looking, but a brother in a rich white neighborhood you know it's gonna raise a few hackles, and with that Stand Your Ground law I could find myself dead."

"Roy, that law wasn't passed until later."

"Brother gets killed, it's Stand Your Ground, later or not. So the owner of the company, she sent Lawton out alone, and when it come time to deliver the stuff, I was there with him."

The two cops walked inside Audrey's bungalow.

"But how did it lead to burgling?"

Roy took the iPad from her lap, swiped his finger, then handed it back to her.

Wanda read out loud: "'Lawton entered the customer's house even though she wasn't home.' Roy? He just *walked* in? Didn't Lawton at least ring the doorbell."

"If you'd read on, you'll find out."

"I wanna know now."

Roy kept an eye on Audrey's bungalow. "The owner she sends Lawton on a visiting appointment. Lawton gets to the lady's mansion and rings the bell. Waits. Tries the door. It's open. So he moseys on in. Finds himself in a walk-in closet. Thinks how Audrey keeps her jewelry in the top drawer. He opens it. Puts all the good stuff in his briefcase and leaves."

"What about the woman?"

"What woman?"

"One he came to see?"

"She stopped Lawton on his way down the road while walking her pooch. They ride back to her house and sells her everything in the catalogue."

"After *robbing* her?"

"Yeah."

"They have sex?"

"I didn't ask."

"Then what happened?"

"We quit the next day."

"That doesn't make sense, Roy."

"What don't make sense?"

"Why would you quit if you could sell everything in the catalogue?"

Roy stared at the glamour puss sitting on the beach. "Wanda, you wanna sell patio furniture all your life or summer in the Hamptons? Fly to Paris when you get the itch, or spend long days in your studio making art while everyone else is sitting behind a desk wondering where their dreams went?"

Roy turned back to Audrey's bungalow. Julia was in the backyard, putting together a café racer she'd been collecting parts for months. He loved the way she crawled over the grass picking up forks, springers, blinkers, and guiding everything into place. She had that inner sense of play all kids have when they reach into the closet, take out their toys, and get lost in creation. Something Roy had seen Wanda do in a YouTube video where she pulled off her studio shelves rubber heads, prosthetic body parts, a pig's nose, putty chins, cheeks, and an assortment of wigs that had had an assortment of lives that she summoned for her art. Both girls so much alike, not even knowing it.

Wanda, unaware of Roy's musing, looked up from his manuscript. "Is Larry an Arabic name?"

"Huh?"

She jabbed his leg. "There's an *Arab* named Larry, here."

"Where?"

"*Here*, in your memoir when you were in Iraq."

"What about him?"

"I've never heard of an Arab named Larry."

"Well there was five hundred Iraqi soldiers surrendered in the desert, all of 'em with the name Mohammed. If you said Mohammed, all of 'em got up. So I gave this one dude, with the big hat, the name Larry." Roy watched Crystal's truck pull alongside his bungalow.

Wanda said, "Where're you going?"

"You just finish reading my memoir and get my movie made." He hurried on down the path and said to Crystal, "Where the hell you been?" Grabbing her by the arm. Taking her inside bungalow.

"I went to Fort Lauderdale with friends."

"*Don't* you bother and tell me?"

"I left you a message, I'd be back in a day or so."

"The money's missing."

"*Let go* of my arm. It *hurts*."

"I don't care. I put the duffel bag under the bed. Locked the bungalow. Now it's gone. You the only other person got the key to the bungalow."

"No, I'm not. The bungalow manager's got duplicates in the office. How do you think Julia gets in, she forgets her key?"

"You say *Julia*?"

"I didn't mean her."

"Didn't mean *what*?"

"Her in particular."

"So Julia stole my money."

"I *didn't* say that."

"But that's what you meant."

"You get on my case like Mama, I'm gonna leave you too."

"Well that's something else I gotta talk to you about."

"What?"

"Your mama."

"What about her?"

"She's *dead*."

The two homicide detectives were now standing at the screen door of Roy's bungalow. He let go of Crystal and said, "That's why *they're* here."

Moments later, Roy came in from the kitchen. The bigger cop waved the drinks away.

"*What?* Y'all don't like coke?"

"Your wife, Roberta LaHood, was shot and killed at the Tote Him Pole Club this afternoon."

"I was already down at the morgue."

"You don't look upset."

"When she was living with Ronnie Harrison, I was."

The smaller cop said, "But not enough to stop you two from robbing the Tote Him Pole Club."

"You have proof I was even *there*, let alone robbed the place?"

"Why did your wife try to kill Ronnie Harrison?"

"*Ask* her."

The bigger cop stepped in. "There was an attempted robbery the other night at Ronnie Harrison's home in Sailfish Point. Your late wife lived at the house and worked at the club. According to everyone we interviewed who worked at the club, they corroborated that Roberta LaHood, your late wife, had the security codes to both places."

Roy laughed. "Obviously Hank Kosinski didn't."

"Whether he did or he didn't, we believe your wife was behind the attempted burglary at Sailfish Point and at the club. The dead woman, Dee Culver, killed at Ronnie Harrison's house, despite the fact that she hadn't worked at the club in years was, obviously, still in communication with your wife and had gotten the security codes from her. And we also believe your late wife was getting a cut for providing them with that information."

Roy said, "Could be. I wouldn't know."

"What do you know?"

"If y'all think Roberta had something to do with the robbery then y'all must know something I don't know, but I haven't been in that club in years, let alone anywhere else. If y'all think I had something to do with it then I'm gonna get my attorney, Jenny Sullivan, to set things straight. She made the D.A. look like a fool once already and she'll do it again if she has to."

The smaller cop said, "Just how familiar was your wife with firearms."

"Tell ya the truth, from what I know not all that much. Maybe she did a whole lot shooting the past five years, but before that I don't remember her ever going to the range."

"If what you say is true, then maybe something else happened."

"What?"

"Your wife may have been murdered."

"Hold on," Roy said. "Y'all just said she tried to rob and kill Ronnie Harrison? Now y'all're saying it's the other way around?"

The bigger cop said, "Look, your wife's gun was locked when Ronnie Harrison shot her. If your wife's intention was to kill him, as Ronnie Harrison claims, then why was it locked?"

"Maybe she forgot to unlock it."

The smaller cop said, "Did she have a habit of doing that?"

"Hell do I know what habits she had? Hadn't seen her in five years. Y'all are the police. Y'all go figure it out." Heading to the front door. "People with half a brain lock their gun if it's loaded, but in the heat of the moment, they could forget to unlock it because of the stress they're under."

The bigger cop said, "Not if it's premeditated. That's what we're trying to get at."

Roy said, "Stress don't care if you're premeditating a crime or not. And with all due respect, the real problem ain't whether she forgot to lock *or* unlock her gun, but the law behind it all. Y'all get that straightened out, y'all won't have to play this game."

"And you'd still be in jail."

Roy stared at the bigger man with the badge, gun, and ego and almost did something he would have regretted.

The smaller cop said, "Did she discuss this with you? Killing Ronnie Harrison."

"*Ask* her."

The bigger cop said, "Maybe you two, for different reasons, were both planning on killing Ronnie Harrison."

"Now why would I wanna kill Ronnie Harrison?"

"He was sleeping with your wife. You already killed Raydel."

"Not for sleeping with my wife."

The smaller cop stepped in. "The point we're trying to get at is, if we can prove your wife didn't have intention to use her gun, then the application of Stand Your Ground would be meaningless in this situation. We could go after Ronnie Harrison for murder, unless you don't give a damn."

"Prove it he murdered her and I'll give a damn. But y'all ain't gonna prove nothing hanging around here," leading them outside. "Your problem ain't with me, gentlemen, but with that law, and until y'all get your heads wrapped around it y'all're just wasting your time trying to pin anything on anyone, because I can cry about my wife getting murdered and y'all can cry about Ronnie Harrison getting away with it and it won't do no one a lick a good. And if y'all still think I murdered Raydel, then read the court documents.

He beat my wife, and when he got bored with that he started stealing her things. Imagine what it does to a woman when she comes home scared like hell. Roberta may not have been a saint, but she didn't deserve to be abused. That's why she bought a gun, and when Raydel found out she got a restraining order on him he told her: 'I'm gonna restrain your ass six feet under.' Unfortunately for him, I was there when he tried. But then I guess y'all missed the second trial, or y'all don't care about abused women. Now, there anything else I can help y'all with?"

The smaller cop said, "We'll be keeping in touch, so don't go anywhere."

"I can go wherever I damn please. In fact, I plan on going to the Hamptons next weekend to swim in Accabonac Bay and eat some sushi with the local potato farmers *if* there's any of 'em left."

Roy waited until the detectives left the colony before taking a quick walk down the path. He pulled up at Audrey's kitchen table, but it was like pulling up before a firing squad. Lawton was all alone on the couch. Julia was outside working on her bike. The sound of her wrenches felt a little too close for Roy.

He said to Audrey, "I thought you didn't want him hanging around here."

"It's my business who hangs around here and my business who leaves."

Julia set the engine in the frame of her café racer. Her hands moved quickly, steadily, and precisely. Somehow Roy felt they were around his neck. He said, "I find it curious the police come over here and then to me. Something y'all needed to tell 'em?"

Audrey said, "I told 'em politely to go to hell."

"Then y'all told 'em I was just down the way."

"They knew exactly where you was, Roy, but they first wanted some information, and obviously they wasn't too pleased with what they got."

"Well, then, I appreciate you saying nothing, but somebody stole my money, and y'all know who it is."

"I don't give a damn, Roy. This whole bungalow colony wants you out of here. Your shenanigans with that girl from New York City have infuriated everyone. They all think it's my fault y'all ran around naked, so they're all asking Billy Pickett, the manager, for me and Julia to quit here. God help you, Roy, should it come down to that."

Julia came in through the beach side of the bungalow and pulled off her tight synthetic mechanic's gloves. "Did you hear from that pool manager, Mama?"

"Yeah, he just called. Said he'd work out a deal to start my swimming school next week. And he picked me over a whole lot of other people too."

"Good." Then to her father. "You're still here?"

Audrey said, "He's gonna need a job. He'll be a good swimming instructor. Taught you well as a child."

"He's already got a job carrying luggage for that Johnson woman." Then to Lawton. "Oh, I forgot; her chauffeur told me to tell you she made supper reservations for eight o'clock. It's a quarter to. Better get over there or else."

"Why didn't you tell me before?"

"Because *I don't* carry your luggage." Turning to Roy, "You here for hotcakes or ice cream?"

Audrey said to Julia, "Somebody here thinks you took something of his."

Julia laughed. "Anybody thinks that can go to hell."

Roy headed to the door.

Julia said with a big grin, "Leaving so early?"

"Two can play this game, Julia."

"A hundred can play this game. So what?"

"You want trouble, young lady? You got it." Roy left the bungalow.

CHAPTER THIRTY-THREE

Mrs. Johnson said to Lawton, "I don't give a damn about any veterans organization. I made reservations for eight o'clock, and you're a half hour late."

"I'm sorry, Kathy, but it's hard to just get up and walk out of a meeting while someone important is speaking."

"And just *who* was speaking?"

"Head of our organization."

"*What* organization?"

"Organization I belong to."

"*What* organization is that?"

"Veterans organization."

"Has it got a name?"

Lawton tried to make himself a drink and then remembered to call the butler. "It's just a local chapter."

Mrs. Johnson said, "Why do you need to go to some organization when you've got someone right here you can talk to?"

"Well, we're all old Ranger buddies, and since you wasn't in the service, it would be kinda hard."

"I don't believe a word you're saying, and it's 'weren't' *not* 'wasn't.'"

"Call 'em up, you don't believe me," pointing to the landline. "Ask for Captain Tom Longfellow."

"I don't have to. Julia told me you spent the whole day with her mother."

"Well, I did stop by for a spell. See, she's starting a business and wanted my advice."

"The hell do you know about business? You're a thief."

The butler arrived and poured Lawton a shot of rye.

"Look, Kathy, why don't we talk about this over supper? I've had a long day."

"*Pursuing* your ex-wife. Or was it some *other* slut?"

There was a hard look on Lawton's face. "I don't think that was necessary."

Mrs. Johnson didn't care. "You said that I'd be wasting my time trying to talk to your little girl. That there'd be no connection. My God were you wrong. There's something big and promising about her, but she's bitter and angry and will need all the help she can get in this unforgiving world, and I don't see you being able to provide any of it. You have no money. No job. No education. Nothing. You're just a small-minded, ignorant middle-aged man who thinks he got lucky all of a sudden. Well, we'll see about that." Mrs. Johnson stormed out of the room.

Lawton spent the rest of the night alone. The next morning a scream brought him to his feet.

CHAPTER THIRTY-FOUR

You did in some bad people, Ronnie, so the law is looking the other way, for now, but don't push your luck; if public pressure continues to mount, they'll go after your ass.

Ronnie woke up. The voice in his dream still heavy on him as he scrolled through the news apps on his phone. The op-eds complained with the baying moan of men and women who in their infinite wisdom feel they're always ignored. One had wondered: *How could the greatest country in the world have the greatest amount of gun violence? Are the twain even synonymous? If so, then to achieve really true greatness what everyone in this country needs is a machine gun instead of a handgun.* Ronnie wasn't so sure about that. He turned over and tried to wake Clarice. She wouldn't budge. He took a glass of water off the night table and drenched her. She woke up shaking like a wet dog. "Ronnie. You're *sick*."

"What happened between Roberta and her husband?"

Wiping herself off. "I told you last night, Ronnie, at the tennis club. Now all of a sudden ya wanna talk about it?"

"I had a lot to drink. *Tell* me again."

"Roberta threw him out first night home."

"*Why?*"

"Hell do I know why?" Burying her head under the pillow, "But if she threw him out, it makes you wonder how they stole the money since they weren't on speaking terms."

Pushing her pillow away, "What do you mean how *they* stole the money?"

"Because all of a sudden she's looking for him. Maybe you killed the wrong person, Ronnie."

"Did Roberta tell you why she threw him out?"

"No," crawling back under the covers.

"Why she was looking for him?"

"Something about Crystal running away from home."

"What happened?"

"Some argument."

"*What* argument?"

"Something Roy LaHood took from Roberta."

"What did he take?"

Clarice said, "Roberta wouldn't tell me. But if I was to see Crystal, to let Roberta know where she was because then she'd know where Roy is and Roberta was desperate to find what he took."

"*Why* was she so desperate?"

"Ronnie, Roberta doesn't tell; she just *orders*."

"You see Crystal a lot?"

"Only in the office, now and then."

"What do you mean 'now and then'?"

"She worked there."

Ronnie asked, "What kinda work?"

Clarice looked out from under the bedsheet. "*You're* asking *me?* It's *your* club, Ronnie. *Not* mine."

"Does she have the security codes to the club?"

"I don't know what Crystal has, but she ran errands for Roberta in the late afternoon when you weren't around. I felt sorry for that kid taking all of Roberta's crap."

"Since when were you there late afternoons?"

"It was *your* idea."

"*What* was my idea?"

"To get Roberta to teach me bookkeeping."

"You learn anything?"

"*No.* I got tired of Roberta's abuse, so I told her I'd rather pole dance than do arithmetic."

Ronnie said, "So then, you're saying LaHood got a hold of my code booklet from Roberta."

"I'm saying he probably got sick of her abuse and robbed you on his own." Clarice rolled over and went back to sleep, but not before saying, "Maybe it's Roy ya oughta talk to."

Ronnie didn't waste any time.

Ronnie had never been to what he considered the poor part of Jensen Beach. The Surfside Bungalow Colony sign, up ahead, had been dulled and clouded by years of wind plus a few nasty hurricanes. It reminded him of the summers he had spent on the Jersey Shore as a kid: rows of cheap motels, flip-flops, endless hours on the beach watching heads bob in the summer heat as seagulls dove in and out of the sky in successive waves. Ronnie parked his car in the lot filled with Pontiacs, Saturns, Chevys, and a Japanese pickup whose visa was up. A '71 Oldsmobile Cutlass Supreme managed to sneak in without any rust. There was a sign up ahead: *A violation sheet will be plastered on your windshield if you drive or park beyond this point.* Ronnie wondered if they'd plaster his car just because it was a Mercedes. He parked and followed a dirt path toward the bungalows. A few of the residents gave Ronnie the eye and wondered if a hotshot real-estate developer had come to calculate how high and expensive he could build after having evicted everyone. Ronnie noticed a pretty girl strolling by on the beach with Roy. Then he saw Julia walk into her bungalow.

Audrey said, "You and I have to talk."
Julia said, "If it's about what I think it is, I'm not interested."
"I just got word your father is in a police station accused of something he didn't do."
"What didn't he do?"
"Steal that old lady's jewelry."
"Mrs. Johnson was *robbed*?"
"Last night."
"What's it gotta do with me?"
"Gertie saw you ride off with Roy's duffel bag this morning; of course she didn't know what's in it."
"Well, finders keepers, losers weepers."
"Julia, we're going to settle this."
"Sure we are, Mama."
"You're going to give the money back to Roy."
"What's that gonna solve?"
"The problem with Mrs. Johnson."
"What problem is that?"
"Roy's the one who robbed her last night, and she thinks it was your father. I want you to give Roy the money he stole from Ronnie, so he'll return the old lady her jewels. Then your father will be released. I want you to think of him, not yourself. The man has just spent ten years in a prison. And I'm not saying this because I love him again, but because it's the right thing to do."
"Where's Roy right now?"
"In yonder quarters, waiting."
"You spoke to him, Mama."
"What do you think?"
"Then that's why she invited me over for supper tonight."

"You told her you'd come?"

"Of course not. I told her I'm busy."

Audrey said, "Call her back and tell her you're coming."

"Mama, I can't stand that woman. She's like a leech that won't let go of me."

Audrey took Julia by the hand and sat her down. "I want you to settle up with this Johnson woman, so we can move on, not make things worse."

Julia said, "We're gonna move on either way." The anger in her eyes stronger than the words spoken.

Ronnie had a feeling maybe he should turn around. Go home. Work this out in his head instead of on the go. Five years in prison lifting weights had put a permanent dent in Roy's physique and Ronnie knew that if he didn't play his cards right, he too would have a permanent dent. He watched Roy and Wanda stroll down the beach. She at times angry. Frustrated. Tossing her head and arms. Using her finger like a stopgap, but every time Roy grabbed her, he kissed her in a way that made her kiss back, which only made her more pissed off. Ronnie knew she hadn't yet wrangled in the thief and it frustrated Wanda who had her own history of using her charm and beauty to swindle attention. She, the art goddess fluent in cozying up to moneyed men and Range Rover women who battled treadmills, Bluetooth devices, therapists, complicated relationships, someone else's children, overeducated dog walkers, Hamptons traffic that was just Manhattan traffic on weekends, and personal trainers who wore spandex that glowed while barking orders under the sheets of someone else's sweat. Wanda was missing New York. The cozy old West Village life. The daily invitations to the endless events that clogged her e-mail from social climbers and well-to-dos if nothing much ado. The stream of visitors to her studio. The collectors, curators, dealers, art writers, and socialites who understood that redemption was not in the art itself nor in the contorted lexicon of postmodernist theory, but in being seen with the people who made it, pun intended. Wanda was also hearing the wailing tick of her biological clock. The frightening thought of being childless overcame her. "Roy, isn't there a time in life when you just want to nest?" Her hand on her tummy as if something little had just kicked, not even thinking of preschool-admission battles, pushy parents whose weapon of choice is backstabbing, or the fact that Roy was a criminal, not some fast-tracking bourgeois with a taste for Tod's Slippers and a weekend farmhouse minus the crop duster.

Roy's first nest had turned into a dungeon. He headed, with zeal, over to the dude with the Mylar sunglasses and soft loafers. Ronnie's slick blue slacks, lime socks, and Ralph Lauren double-weave piqué yellow polo shirt with the porterhouse-size polo player logo that made him about as colorful as a circus tent. He trundled on with the puffy jowls and sloppy feet of a dishwasher aboard a sinking ship. Roy turned back to Wanda. "*Stay* where you are."

Not according to Wanda.

Roy said, "There's a fat dude over there who's killed four people in the past two days. I don't want you to be number five."

"I don't want you to be number six."

Roy gulped. "I didn't know you cared so much," and tossed her in the ocean.

Ronnie didn't miss the move. The big tall man, in board shorts, now heading toward him with giant strides. Ronnie wanted to run, not because he was scared, even though he was, but this was supposed to be a dress rehearsal to get the feel of all the schlubs in the bungalow colony before making his real move on Roy the killer. Ronnie planned on telling the judge, after he took Roy down, that he had gone to visit an old employee, a Ms. Julia Gibbs, who had money owed, and then out of nowhere, a scary six-feet-six Afro dude tries to kill him, who just happens to be the same dude who had been sent up to Starke for murder. He was sure the judge would understand, because the people who passed the Stand Your Ground law knew what it was like to live in a dangerous, scary, savage-ridden land of crazies, often referred to as the "United States," where if you weren't armed to the teeth, the boogey man would get you right out the front door, despite the fact that the boogey man was, more often than not, the one walking out that front door.

Roy put Ronnie's plan on permanent hold. "You come here to make it number five, Mr. Harrison?"

Ronnie played dumb. "Excuse me, sir, I have no idea what you're talking about."

Roy could play dumb too. "Neither do I. See, I got amnesia. Been suffering it the day my wife was murdered. Remember Roberta? Or you got amnesia too?"

Ronnie pressed his right hand against his hip to make sure his Glock hadn't slipped away while getting out of his Mercedes. "Excuse me, sir, but I came here to visit an old employee of mine," trying to squirm past Roy, having no luck. "There's money owed her, and she deserves every cent of it."

"Funny thing about amnesia," Roy said. "The one thing you never forget is an asshole. And I haven't forgotten you," surprised at how the photos of Ronnie online looked no different than the man in front of him, like the pickles once served at Wolfie's that looked the same no matter what time of year it was.

Ronnie was now facedown in the grass with a lot of dirt up his nose. His Glock in Roy's waistband. Roy said, "Let me tell you something, fatso; you left my daughter without a mother, and now she thinks it's my fault you killed her despite the fact the last time Roberta drew a gun it was with a crayon." Lifting Ronnie off the ground like dog poop,. "You try that Stand Your Ground bullshit with me, muthafucka, I will come after your white ass and carve it up like lox on a bagel. You *do* know what a bagel is?" Ronnie nodded his head up and down like a lifeless puppet. "Good. Now get the fuck outta here or you gonna be swimming with the fishes."

Pointing to the broad Atlantic, just a stone's throw away, where Wanda stood under sky-high palm trees watching all the action. Roy dragged Ronnie to his white Mercedes and stuffed him in like dirty laundry. He took off. Clouds of dirt kicked up the air. Wanda, always seeing things in the context of art, hollered from under the wishbone of two overlapping palm trees, "Roy, are you familiar with post-postmodernism?"

"Why—? *Should* I be?"

CHAPTER THIRTY-FIVE

The late-afternoon sun left a golden glow with long animated shadows that stalked bathers leaving the beach. Bold colored towels, folding chairs, white Styrofoam coolers, little plastic shovels and pails, and bright colored beach balls were carried or dragged to the parking lot. Mothers bundled small children behind opened car doors and changed them into dry clothing as their little feet danced in the open space and not so happily. A man, on the other side of the beach, rode a scooter through the bungalow colony's dirt path, and from the shore the two-wheeler sounded like a bee. The man cut the ignition and approached Roy's bungalow. He wore a dark gray suit, black tie, and a white dress shirt. His hands were in front of him, one over the other, as if he'd been laid to rest. He was of average height with eyes that didn't challenge. His demeanor was more like a museum guard who reminds you, with a white glove, where you should be without threatening where you might end up. Roy opened the front door of his tiny bungalow. The visitor said, "We are Clemens."

Roy looked over the man's shoulders and couldn't find anyone else. "*We—?*"

"Yes, sir," the notion of *I* having been expelled. "Mrs. Johnson would like to have the pleasure of your company." Clemens swept his arm toward the two-wheeler just down the path.

Roy saw a cream-colored Vespa. "That yours?"

"Yes, sir."

"What happened to the Bentley?"

"Williams is washing it, sir."

"Who's he?"

"The washer."

"Who are you?"

"The butler. We met at the house. Don't you remember, sir?"

"Why didn't Mrs. Johnson send the chauffeur?"

"He's busy washing the Bentley."

"Maybe y'all don't think I rate a Bentley."

"As you wish, sir." Clemens put on his helmet and headed toward the Vespa.

Roy yelled over the butler's head, "I gotta ride on that?"

Clemens snapped on his chinstrap and mounted the two-wheeler. "You'll find it most comfortable, sir."

"What if I'm busy and can't come?"

Clemens held the other helmet up in the air. "You weren't too busy last night, sir."

The Vespa stopped just short of a magnificent red barn that had enough brass and recycled iron to be sufficiently old and yet ardently modern. Roy hopped off and stared at the horses grazing in yonder field under the shade of tall turkey oaks that towered into the sky. He turned to Clemens, "I gotta get on a horse now?"

"You'll find Mrs. Johnson just inside the stable, sir."

"Yeah, but I don't know nothing about horses."

"Don't worry, sir. They know nothing about you," as he redirected himself toward the main house. Roy entered the barn, but it wasn't one of rafter owls, pitchforks, or Minneapolis Moline B G 1 wide row crops. Here the architects clashed over wood species, region of quarry, tone of paint, position of cupola, Dove of Peace, whether or not to build into a closed ring or create an open pathway of Kentucky roses and white lilies with lawn jockeys guiding the way with lanterns. And then there was the footing. Should it be of sand, topsoil, or rubber? Or wood, rubber, sand, peat moss, or maybe Kate Moss? Each school of thought was considered, and as in wine tasting, there was a lot of sniffing and tongue slurping. The tenants, exempt from consultation, poked their heads out of their air-conditioned stalls and took stock of the tall man entering their billet who might soon be on their back. A few turned away and showed their hindquarters. Others nodded their heads up and down expecting a carrot. The rest chewed on their bales of hay or buckets of feed. Roy noticed a light toward the middle of the barn coming from the tack room. As he approached it, Mrs. Johnson appeared wearing full-seat britches and russet cavalry field boots all the way up her calves. Her white blouse was muddied with streaks of muck up to her elbows. She wiped her hands on a towel. Tossed it on a hook and said to her guest, "The dentist was here."

"You got a toothache?"

Mrs. Johnson said, "I'm the one who held his head."

"*Whose?*"

"Wilbur's."

"*Wilbur?*"

"The one who had his tooth pulled," pointing to Wilbur, who was across the way with his rear to them. His tail relentlessly swiping at a fly buzzing over his hocks.

Mrs. Johnson said, "Do you know anything about horses, Roy?"

Stepping back in fear. "My teeth are fine."

Mrs. Johnson laughed and led Roy out the barn. He had expected her to be cross, but she beamed as if good news had just arrived. They passed the open riding ring, where a row of red-and-white fences were stacked in twos and threes down and across past a Liverpool by the center stacked five. Roy said, "You jump them fences?"

"Of course."

"How do you get the pony over it?"

Mrs. Johnson said, "The same way you get into someone's house and take their jewels."

They continued on down to the pool patio and stopped at a round table with an open umbrella that had a design of interlocking golden horseshoes that spelled Johnson. A pitcher of lemonade and imported soda water were aligned with a bucket of ice and assorted liquor. Mrs. Johnson said, "Please, have a seat."

Roy sunk into his chair and took in the grand estate spread out before him. He fantasized it was his: The yonder three-hole golf course with nary a divot. The long, sleek 165-foot yacht loaded in the water with bow-to-stern tinted windows and an antenna capable of contacting Mars. The ship had double top decks: one for swimming, the other for vertical landings. Roy was dreaming of morning splashes in the Aegean. Skiing the Alps in the afternoon. Dancing under the evening Bali moon. Or just riding the surf off Sullivan's Island with a lunch of shrimp and crab-finger scampi awaiting ashore. He poured a glass of Chablis grand cru and let the thought drift away, knowing it wasn't going far. He turned to Mrs. Johnson, whose long, angular fingers nibbled at the top button of her blouse. She looked fuller, stronger, feral, if not younger. There seemed to be a connection between power and vitality, one feeding the other, and when seen at the right angle, it appeared nearly ageless. Roy was pleased he had come, pleased to be surrounded by the finer things of life. He said, "You look very nice," realizing age unlike youth held memories that needed to be revived before taking leave of this world.

"Thank you, Roy," moving closer to him.

Roy was thinking Mrs. Johnson had that way women have when they suddenly become interested in you. Their eyes brighten. Their gaze strengthens. You become the only thing in their world.

Roy said, "I do apologize for last night. You understand that it wasn't personal and that I hold the highest respect for you as always."

"At first I wanted to destroy you."

"That is understandable, Kathy."

"But I always recover from my baser emotions. Reason allows options unavailable in a rage. So, I'm not angry at you at all."

Roy said, "Then you're interested in the trade I mentioned on the phone."

"I might be. But Lawton is down at the police station, and he'll be staying there unless it's of real interest to me."

"It has to do with Julia," Roy said. "She gives me what I want, I give you what you want."

"What exactly did Julia take from you?"

"Something worth a lot of money."

"How much?"

"Enough so that I had to take your jewels, so we could make an exchange, and you did exactly as I had planned."

"Yes, but what did she take?"

"As I said, a lot of money. Julia returns what's mine then you get your jewels. Again, nothing personal."

"So," Mrs. Johnson mused, "I just happen to have been conveniently useful."

"Yes."

"And you won't tell me exactly what she took?"

"With all due respect, ma'am, you did speak to Julia."

"Yes."

"She didn't tell you?"

"No. But I'm having her over for supper, and I'm going to give her something that will make her give back whatever it is you're missing, and maybe then she'll have the good grace to tell me."

"It's just some money I put aside before I went to prison," Roy said. "That's what she took."

"So she's following in her father's footsteps."

"No, ma'am, she's just being a pain in the ass."

"I see. Then no more is to be said." Mrs. Johnson arose. "Do you bathe?"

"Why, every day."

"You misunderstand me, Roy."

Roy watched as she unbuttoned the rest of her shirt. He was more than stunned when she undid her bra and dropped it over her chair. "You're really not angry with me for taking your jewels?"

With a tight spicy smile, "*These* are my jewels." Tugging down her tight riding britches. Diving into the pool and swimming to the other side, "The water's lovely. Please. Come in."

"Ma'am. Do you know what you're doing?"

"Roy, *get* in the water."

Roy stripped and dove into the bright, shiny pool that diffused the sunlight into thousands of tiny reflective facets that lit up the water.

He was treading right beside her. "You *sure* you wanna do this?"

Touching his shoulders. Looking into his eyes. "You mean the exchange?"

"I mean something else." Wondering if he would be eaten alive.

CHAPTER THIRTY-SIX

Clemens brought Julia into the dining room and seated her. There were no predinner drinks, no idle chatter. A sterner and colder air had replaced the warmth from the day before. Mrs. Johnson said, "Jewelry was stolen from this house last night, because of you, but I've been assured that it will be returned tomorrow afternoon at four o'clock so that all charges may be dropped against your father. If not, I assure you, several people will be going to prison, including you."

"For what?"

"Don't interrupt me. Roy stopped by this afternoon. We had a long talk. I like him. He gets right to the point. Knows what he wants. Doesn't hold a grudge. Men like him I understand. He simply desires money and has little use for honors, prizes, fame, and the need to be remembered by this miserable world long after he's gone. People like him are always useful. Not because they can be bought, but because their price is never attached to a self-image, which is always hostage to a more inflated value. In fact, I would have done as he had done had I been in the same situation;

notwithstanding that, I am one who prefers to find opportunity in a crisis, not hold a grudge." She leaned in to make her point. "You will return what you took from Roy and have it here by four o'clock tomorrow and in exchange for my jewelry, I'm going to give you something that will change your life forever and hopefully—your opinion of me."

"What are giving me?"

"Influence."

"*Influence?*"

"*My* influence."

"I still don't understand."

"Do you know what a lobbyist is?"

"Why are you asking me that?"

Leaning back like a scholar steering a colloquium into the finer points of quantum theory, Mrs. Johnson expounded, "Because lobbyists and special interest groups worm their way through the revolving doors of government and business. They can be moderately paid Treasury officials who move on as highly paid bankers, or congressional staffers who find lucrative work in industry; and because they know the right people in government and how to grease the wheels of Congress, they get paid a fortune. That was how the banking deregulation was completed by my husband and his men, and that is how all legislation and affairs of business and art are done: out of favors and influence, all what you've been reading online about my late husband, Leyland. And *you*, my dear, desperately need both; so, in return for Roy's money that you stole, you'll go to Harvard College this fall. Pack your bags. Your life is about to radically change." Mrs. Johnson waited for the excited response.

Instead, Julia felt numb. She thought of Ronnie. All his talk about influence. Duke. The right college with the right people, as if anyone could be right in this hypocritical, self-serving, delusional world of people too messy and demanding and too depleting in the face of ambition, ideology, and that all-consuming worm: self-interest.

Mrs. Johnson said, "You *did* hear me?"

"I have ears."

"*Good.* When you graduate, you will make more money than the piddling amount that Roy wants returned. And if you prefer to be a doctor or researcher, you will satisfy every scientific yearning you've ever had, and you will accomplish things no other person has. That is how much I believe in you and your abilities, and that is why I'm giving you the keys to the world, but if you choose to be an activist on this matter, you'll end up with nothing. So be smart, mature, and understand that this is more than just an offer. It is a way out of your miserable little situation—a situation, which I admit, you have proven to have handled quite adeptly despite the fact that it has turned you into an irritable, ornery, and bitter girl, which I do believe will soon wear out once you matriculate into the rarified world of Cambridge. You are young and brilliant. You have the right temperament for leadership. You are daring, but not without caution. Fearless, but not without reflection. Self-aware and beautiful."

"Just how will you pull this off?"

"Pull what off?"

"Harvard."

"Legacy."

"Huh?"

"Influence."

"*More* of that?"

"Yes. And *learn* to accept it. I have the power to get you into Harvard even if you're a dunce. I will loan you the money. A quarter of a million. You'll get it interest-free with twenty-five years to pay it off. I'll be dead by then. Not a bad deal."

"I still don't understand."

"*What* don't you understand?"

"This legacy business."

Mrs. Johnson paused as she took in the extent of the girl's ignorance. "You *have* heard of the Kennedys or the Bush family?"

"What about them?"

"My kin and theirs and those of other rich, powerful families may go to Harvard, Yale, or wherever, if they should so desire, regardless of their grades or intelligence because of legacy enrollment. It's what's known as 'American exceptionalism.'"

"It *is*?"

"With exceptions."

"Were you going to do this for me anyway," Julia said, "or is this just guilt over what I said to you yesterday? Because you barely know me, despite all your accusations."

"Well you can't say that I haven't tried to get to know you." Mrs. Johnson rang the dinner bell. The servants entered and inaugurated dinner. The business of dining and light conversation took over.

CHAPTER THIRTY-SEVEN

The following afternoon the sky was blotted with huge white cotton cumulus that formed a steep billowy range extending as far as the eye could see and as wide as the sun could reach. The heat had been rising all morning and hung heavily over the Florida eastern seaboard, but further out the ocean was deep blue in the extended mist and purple just beyond. Empty tankers lay low and still on the horizon. A cruise ship, stacked high, was off to the Bahamas. Speed boats skipped over water. Sailboats in the wind pitched at a steep angle. On shore, the beach was too hot to stand, so Roy, quick on his feet, dropped a towel and got under the sun with everyone else. "Mind if I join you?"

"You already have," Audrey said. "Where's your friend?"

"On her way to LA. Some big collector's having some kinda soireée in her honor. How'd dinner go with Julia and the old lady last night?"

"Julia was up and out before I got up."

"Well, I got good news," Roy said.

"What?"

"Now that Roberta's dead, my house is legally all mine. I'll be sleeping at home starting tonight."

"Good. You haven't seen Julia?"

"Not since yesterday. Why?"

"It's already past one," Audrey said. "One of the better colleges called and said she's been accepted for the fall. They got a good scholarship program with an excellent medical school, and it's affordable. They can't wait to have her as a student and if she misses this opportunity, it will be a very sad day for her."

"What's the problem?"

"The admissions office tried her mobile phone and she didn't answer."

"Battery could be dead. You know how them kids use the phone."

"I'm worried."

"Mamas always worry."

"It's not like Julia."

"You told the school she wants to go?"

"Yes, but she has to call back," Audrey said. "The semester starts next week and Julia has a lot to do."

"Her mother's word ain't good enough?"

"They want to hear from *her*, Roy."

"I think you're making a mountain out of a mole hill. If she's accepted, she's accepted."

"Not if she won't call back."

"Tell ya what. When I see Julia at the old lady's, I'll tell her about the college and have her call from there. Schools stay open till at least five."

"I'm coming along, Roy."

"*Where?*"

"To the old lady's."

Roy brushed off some sand, ready to take in the sun. "I don't know if she'd like you being there, the ex-wife of you know who."

"I don't give a damn what she likes. Julia's *my* little girl, not hers. Now get the keys to Crystal's truck."

"She took it," Roy said, "and I don't know where she went."

"Then I'll borrow Billy Pickett's truck."

"Who's he?"

"Manager of the colony that wants you the hell outta here or didgya forget already?"

"Look, Audrey, I don't think it's wise you going, and I ain't trying to be mean or nothing."

"When I want your advice, I'll ask for it," getting up, collecting her beach things.

"*Hey*, I just got here."

"I gotta get bail for Lawton."

"Bail? I thought the police just wanted to talk to him," shaking out his towel.

"Turns out they want more than that."

"Well, he won't need bail," Roy said. "He gonna be free in a few hours."

"I wouldn't be so sure of that."

Slipping on his T-shirt. Adjusting his shades. "What if that old lady won't let you in her mansion?"

"Since you're so good at getting in places, you'll find me a way."

Audrey knocked on Billy Pickett's office door and got the keys to his truck.

CHAPTER THIRTY-EIGHT

Clarice reached for the sunscreen on the pool deck. "Only someone stupid leaves a million-five in their basement," and sprayed.

Ronnie was at the edge of the pool, keeping an eye on his yacht. Some kids snuck on the other day and left a mess. The police came over, but said they needed a body, not joints and empty beer bottles to prosecute. This time Ronnie wasn't going to let the little bastards get away.

Clarice hollered from her lounge chaise. "There's nobody down there, Ronnie," picking out a bothersome piece of ice from her cocktail. Looking for a snack. "I thought the maid was coming out with grilled shrimp and tuna salad?"

"I find those kids screwing on my yacht, again, I'm gonna screw 'em for good." Worried they'd find the money hidden in the lower-deck bedroom's secret cabinet.

"Yeah, Ronnie. Like ya screwed Roy LaHood yesterday? Or should I say like he screwed you."

"Clarice, you forget about those four other people thought they could screw me."

"Look, Ronnie," trying to take his side, "I'd hate it too, I lost three million dollars."

"You never had three million, so how would you know?"

"That's why I'd hate it."

Ronnie, patting his empty hip. "My gun is legal and registered. LaHood uses it, he's fucked."

"I don't know about that. You go after him and he stands his ground, you're the one who's fucked."

Ronnie turned to Clarice, comfy in her chaise like she was married to him. "Roy LaHood uses my gun, he goes back to jail for the rest if his life. Ask Buford."

Clarice reached for a grilled shrimp the maid had just brought out. "So far that LaHood has been pretty smart. Maybe he's waiting for ya to do something dumb, like try and kill him again."

Ronnie came over and pushed the shrimp tray away. "How come you never take my side?"

"Because I ain't stupid. I may not add so fast, but I can think. I know what goes on and without me you'd still be scratching your head wondering who stole your three million and left ya broke."

"I got way more hidden away where nobody can get his hands on it."

"Ya mean that bank in Antigua?"

"Who told you about that?"

Clarice laughed. "Everybody knows about it and it's run by a guy who's in love with Julia."

"Just what are you saying?"

"I'm saying if one day all your money disappears, who're ya gonna complain to?"

"Whaddya mean?"

"You're gonna dig up J. Edgar Hoover?"

"Offshore banks don't steal your money. Only onshore ones like Wall Street."

Clarice reached over and popped another shrimp in her mouth. "How much money do ya really have off shore, Ronnie?"

"Why do *you* want to know?"

"Because if ya got twenty million, what's three? If all ya got is three thousand, then I'd be pissed. How much ya got tucked away, Ronnie?"

"I think you're missing the point."

"Ronnie, I don't miss as much as ya think."

"It's not the money."

"What is it then?"

"I don't like anybody taking advantage of me."

"Well, Ronnie, if ya go after this LaHood, you're *really* fucked. Now, how much money ya got including all your assets, what they call '*hard* assets'?"

Ronnie sat down with his new accountant. "What's it your business?" Kicking away his schnauzer who thought tuna salad was some new kind of dog food.

"Roberta told me you're worth at least twenty million in hard assets and other investments over the years or is that all bullshit?"

Ronnie stopped chewing on a shrimp and played dumb. "*What* other investments?"

Clarice said, "The ones Roberta use to tell everyone about when she got angry with ya. But that's not what I'm really getting at, Ronnie. What I'm really getting at is—are you a rational person?"

"Of course, I'm rational," reaching for the more crispy shrimp before Clarice got it.

"Then who cares about the three million?"

"*I* fucking do."

"Ronnie, ya wipe away four people and get away with it. That's not bad. Okay, so ya missed Roy LaHood yesterday, but you're still batting four for five and Joe DiMaggio never did that. .408 tops and nobody's done better since and I'm talking 1941."

"You're suddenly a baseball statistician?"

"No, but my uncle Alton wouldn't shut up about Joltin' Joe and all his numbers. Look Ronnie, maybe I can't add as fast as Roberta, but I always quit when I'm ahead. Fuck the three million."

Ronnie stared at Clarice, now the big macher with all the know-how. He said, "You just want me to forget *three* million dollars?"

"All I'm saying is be rational. You got ten, twenty million? You're way ahead of the game. Unless all ya really got is three thousand."

"You forget that nigger over in Jensen Beach is laughing his head off at me and I don't fucking like it."

"Let him laugh," Clarice said. "You're business is dead. No one is ever going to your club again, let alone work for ya. They're screaming their heads off on TV and online: *Club owner blows away his staff.* Ya know what I'm thinking, Ronnie?"

"What?"

Clarice got up and looked for her top. "You're a lucky guy and don't even know it."

"I don't care. I want my three million back."

"Go after LaHood and he'll kill ya."

"He'll go to jail if he does."

"And *you'll* be in the cemetery," fastening her top. "I ask you again. *Are you* a rational person?"

"Fuck rational. I stood my ground before. I'll do it again."

"Sure, Ronnie. But from now on, wherever ya stand, you're on a pile of shit." She put on her sandals and headed toward the garage with her bag slung over her shoulder.

"Where the hell're you going?"

"Home, Ronnie."

"Why?"

"I gotta think about this relationship before going any further." She disappeared behind the hedges.

CHAPTER THIRTY-NINE

Audrey steered Billy Pickett's Dodge Ram into the long driveway of Mrs. Johnson's estate, where in the spill and splatter of steel and glass a house appeared whose ego, like the person who'd designed it, was so huge it had to be strapped in or risk exploding.

Audrey parked by the entrance of the front door, or what appeared to be a front door, and said to Lawton, "You wait here in the truck. *Do not* leave until I return. And *do not* smoke. Billy wants his truck clean."

Lawton, holding an unlit cigarette near his mouth. "It could be a long time."

"I don't care it's ten years. I paid your bail with the money going for Julia's college education and I plan on getting every god damn cent of it back."

Roy was about to say something, but he knew better. He followed Audrey to the foot of the front door. Clemens appeared and showed them into the private living room, where Mrs. Johnson was seated on a long mist leather sofa that peeled off like a wave. She was more than surprised to see Audrey, but graciously accepted her presence. She offered them chairs opposite hers. Roy sat down, but his eyes were fixed on the long glass walls. The house at first impression had seemed cold, narrowly functional, void of any sensitivity, but now with prison a week behind him, the scent of premium leather and exotic wood against the gloss of extended walls that funneled volumes of light into a world so unlike lockup, he thought it must be beautiful on some level, if still violently cold and raw, like a dictator's vision that demanded appreciation or death; and as with all the houses he and Lawton had cat burgled over the years, he wondered why so many rich people had so little soul, or was it just easier to accumulate objects than it was character, which was better than being poor and accumulating neither. Still, it was a place he could move into on a moment's notice.

Mrs. Johnson, unaware of the thief's assessment, turned to Audrey with a formality meant to keep frivolity and cheap chatter at bay. "Please do not think of me as being rude, Mrs. Gibbs; just what brings you here?"

"*You* Mrs. Johnson."

Mrs. Johnson didn't like the tone of the younger woman's voice. There was something unnerving about the way she said *You*, as if all her grievances were attached to it. Worse, the younger woman didn't see herself as a guest, but inconvenienced, as if she had been ticketed and summoned to court.

"Lawton mentioned to me that you're starting your own business."

"I am."

"How delightful. Something about a swimming school?"

"Yes."

"Were you a national champion?"

"No."

"Did you compete in college?"

"Never went to college."

"I was on the equestrian team."

"I wasn't," Audrey said.

"No, but you grew up on a horse farm."

"Yes."

"You're Southern, like I am."

"Yes."

"We have something in common."

"I suppose." Letting Mrs. Johnson know she was wasting her time trying to get close.

Not one to be discouraged, Mrs. Johnson again tried to engage the younger woman, who seemed to be unaffected by fine taste, grand living, and the American notion of aristocracy expressed not in knighthoods and baronies, but in measurements: 1 percent being the highest title at the moment. "I see so much of Julia in you. In fact, I find the resemblance stunning. From whom did she get her blond hair? "

"Lawton's mother."

"Is she still alive?"

"Dead."

"Would you like a drink?"

"No."

Mrs. Johnson turned to Roy. "How about you? You never turn down a drink."

"I'm fine, like the lady."

Mrs. Johnson envied how the younger woman governed her men with an inner strength not easily decipherable nor transmittable. Clearly, Lawton had chosen well. Mrs. Johnson said, "If y'all should want anything, please feel free to ask." Her mind really on Julia, so hard to get out of her head. Thinking the girl's orneriness was more like larva before turning into a full-fledged women, something Mrs. Johnson had been deprived of by culture and generation. With nothing more to say, they sat there for twenty minutes, at first uncomfortably, and then pacified by the silence.

Mrs. Johnson, sensing it was late, checked her Cartier Ballon Bleu. "It's twenty after four. Where's Julia?"

Clemens appeared with a square envelope the color of a peach. It didn't escape Mrs. Johnson that it matched the leather sofa that she and Julia had sat on the day before in her study. A clever touch, she thought, and a hint of good news.

At the same time, 1,177 nautical miles east of Jupiter Island, a PAC 750 approached Antigua with a crosswind that hammered the roller door. The pilot raised his voice and spoke over the deafening airstream. "St. John's Harbor is right up ahead, Julia."

She pointed leeward. "I want the undeveloped side off the main inlet."

"We're approaching it now."

Julia checked the duffel bag attached to the static line and moved it toward the roller door. "I'm ready, Bob."

The pilot banked east off the ocean and leveled out just under eight thousand feet, more than high enough so that no one could read the letter markings with the naked eye.

Julia pushed the duffel bag out the roller door. She followed, free-falling. Her eyes steady on her analog altimeter watch. Her descent a knife-slicing plummet. The world coming at her like a fist. At one thousand feet, she pulled the ripcord and snapped out of her dive. In seconds, she touched ground. The duffel bag following moments later. Her phone going off in her hip pocket.

Ronnie, alone by the pool. The Atlantic Ocean spread out before him, like lunch. "Julia?"

"What is it, Ronnie?" Looking down the long empty road that led to town.

"Your mother's looking for you. Said you got into some college."

"That's not why you called."

"Where are you? You sound out of breath."

"I'm busy, Ronnie," watching the PAC 750 head home.

"I just called to tell you, you're a smart girl, Julia. You'll do well wherever you go."

"Thanks, Ronnie," gathering up her parachute.

"I just got rid of Clarice."

"What took so long?"

"You know how it is. You doing anything tonight?"

"I'm *busy*, Ronnie. *Don't* you listen?"

"I was just thinking."

"You're always just thinking," folding the parachute.

"I mean, if you're not doing anything, I was just thinking we could, you know. I'm kinda lonely."

"Get some of the other girls to come over."

"You don't want to see me again?"

"I didn't say that."

"You can captain the yacht, tonight, if you want. You're the boss. I don't care you tip it over and it sinks."

"Can't, Ronnie," looking at the sky so wide she could see it curve around the horizon.

"Julia, you're not listening to all the bullshit the media's saying?"

"Well, they haven't asked my opinion," heading toward the duffel bag.

"Look, Julia, I'm a little dazed from what dumbbell Marty and Roberta tried to pull. I mean, I walk into my place of business, and they try to kill me."

"Sure, Ronnie," dragging the duffel bag and parachute to clearer ground.

"Believe what you want, Julia, but this time I talk to the media and do a thirty-minute interview about the whole thing and the assholes edit it down to twelve seconds of air time. You call that *fair*?"

"You were asked about the Stand Your Ground law, Ronnie, and you said: 'There are a lot of people who don't deserve to live.'"

"Yeah, but I said that *before* they asked me the question. I said people like Hitler didn't deserve to live and we paid for it. The media fucked me over."

"You expect them not to?"

"I expect them to be fair."

"Then you don't live in the real world, Ronnie. The news is about ratings, not news. Otherwise TV personalities wouldn't be getting million-dollar salaries for telling you it's going to be sunny tomorrow, unless you're dumb enough to believe paying them a normal salary means it's *always* going to rain. By the way, I hear you went after Roy," folding the second parachute.

"Julia, all I did was to stop by to give you the money I owed you and that dick pulls some stunt on me."

"Yeah, but you don't owe me anything."

"Look, I was in the neighborhood, and I—"

Julia lowered the phone from her ear and searched the long, empty road that only the sun could find.

Ronnie, still talking. "I mean, if you weren't so young, Julia, look, we're two adults. Why do we have to let age get between us?"

Putting the phone back to her ear. Trying to end the conversation. "Ronnie, if it weren't age, it would be something else. So don't kid yourself."

"But I love you."

"Sure and if I were ugly you'd hate me," stacking the parachutes on top of each other. "Look, I got a new boyfriend, and he's right here. So, like, I can't talk right now."

"Oh."

"I gotta go."

"You called the dean back?"

"Yeah, all kinds of numbers to press and a zillion recorded voices. Drove me nuts. Then she finally picks up. I gotta go, Ronnie," and cut him off.

A plain rented car came trundling down the long, desolate road and pulled alongside Julia. The passenger door opened. Crystal leaned over and pushed her jump gear to the backseat. She helped Julia lug in the duffel bag and parachutes.

Julia said, "For a second I thought you weren't coming."

"Why would you think that?"

Thinking of Ronnie. "When you're all alone, you think those things."

"Well, you're not all alone." They rode off to the bank.

Mrs. Johnson took the envelope and the letter opener off the silver tray. She slit the sealed flap and pulled out the note. Julia's voice was loud and clear:

Dear Miss Kathy,
    Ronnie Harrison used to always tell me people who do you favors always expect something in return and that people who give you something of exceptional value will invariably think they own a piece of you. From what I've seen, you own too much for me to think otherwise, and though I may be wrong, I cannot risk that I'm not; therefore, I reject your offer, but not the time spent with you.
With much love,
Julia

Roy could see the disappointment in the old woman's face as she finished reading the note. She handed it to him. Roy read it and left it on the coffee table, along with her jewels. "Ya win some. Ya lose some."

He and Audrey left.

Mrs. Johnson, alone again, looked out beyond her house, once a bright lantern that faced the sea. Something was washing ashore and enveloping the island. It was as inky and slick as the early evening and as blue as the feeling of something won then lost.

CHAPTER FORTY

A month later.

Ronnie's new girlfriend, Wynona, was losing her patience. "Look, Ronnie, I been going out with you since the beginning of September and not once can I ride on your boat. I'm beginning to wonder if it's yours at all, or are you just waiting for the next hurricane, so we can drown?" They were out on the pool deck with drinks. The sun already down. An early October chill gripped the air. "Why didn't you hire the last captain the agency sent over? He had a real nice smile and wasn't old."

Ronnie said, "I'm the one supposed to be smiling, not the captain."

"Well, I'm getting tired sitting out here every night looking at your boat, never getting a ride. The way the climate is changing, it just might snow next week."

The newly hired maid and cook came out with supper on a rolling tray and set the grilled shrimp and tuna salad on the patio table.

Wynona groaned, "Grilled shrimp and tuna salad, again? You eat the same thing every day."

Ronnie said to the cook, "Make her a steak."

"I don't want steak."

"What do you want?"

"I wanna go on that boat. If we can't ride on it, let's at least eat on it."

Ronnie said, "I gotta get the power going. Set the kitchen up. It's a long walk from here. By then the shrimp will be cold."

"Then I'll have a few drinks and wait." Turning to the cook. "Make me some veal parmigiani."

The cook said, "We don't have any veal, ma'am."

"There's chicken tenders in the refrigerator," Wynona said. The cook and maid went back to the kitchen. "Where ya going, Ronnie?"

"To the fucking boat so you can eat your chicken tender parmigiani."

She hollered, "Maybe ya oughta get a sailboat, Ronnie. At least you won't have to worry about turning on the power."

Ronnie wondered why he always ended up with the same kind of girl. He pulled out his phone and tried Julia again. He got the same recorded message and hung up. He walked up the gangplank to his yacht and made his way below deck and down the hall toward an annoying noise coming from the forward deck: the sound of someone laughing at his expense. Ronnie opened the stateroom door. Two kids were doing it on the big master bed. Ronnie recognized the boy. Tall and gawky and blue from all the effort. Long dark hair that always looked wet and dirty. He had flat poolroom eyes used to low light and whispers: a pose acquired as a result of always being on the lookout, except for now. The girl under him was of shy soft eyes and struggling to get out of adolescence. Somehow she thought the boy's schemes would help, but not anymore. She threw her arms over her chest and revealed body art of sparrows, roses, and two little mermaids. Ronnie said to the boy, "How many times have I thrown you off my boat?"

The kid, now on his back. "You lay a hand on me, you'll be in big trouble with my father." Ronnie noticed the short pipe that wasn't for smoking Prince Albert Crimp Cut. The liquor stains and other excretions on the carpet. Joints mashed into his expensive furniture. Underwear, shoes, all over the place dorm room style. The kid said, "Look, like, I'm sorry, dude." Pointing to his new girlfriend. "She wanted to see what it was like inside a boat."

"I *never* said that."

The kid pushed her aside and said to Ronnie, "Your maid can clean this up in no time. I gotta go. My dad's gonna be looking for me. You don't wanna know what he's like when he's pissed."

Ronnie said, "How old are you?"

"Twenty-one."

"Your father couldn't give a shit where you are." Ronnie told the girl, arms still over her chest, "Get out."

She took whatever clothing she could grab and ran.

Ronnie walked over to the kid. "Get off the fucking bed."

"You lay a hand on me, my father will kill you."

Ronnie said, "Hit me in the face."

"*What?*"

There was a madness in Ronnie's eyes. The kind a vulture has when it circles the dead.

The kid, standing on the floor, swung at Ronnie. Ronnie fell against the door. "Pick up the fucking vase."

"Why?"

"Throw it at me."

The kid threw the vase. It hit Wynona as she walked in the bedroom.

"The fuck's going on, Ronnie?"

Ronnie fired his new Glock at the kid. "I'm standing my ground is what the fuck's going on."

CHAPTER FORTY-ONE

Several days later.

Roy was trying to convince Audrey that they should try selling swimming and surfing lessons to his old robbery victims. He said, "Every one of 'em is fine family people who love their children and would appreciate the philosophy of your school."

Audrey added, "Just not as much as you appreciated their jewelry," but thinking his idea did have some merit. "In the meantime, I want y'all to video each kid. They learn quicker when they see their mistakes."

"What about my idea?"

Audrey knew there was always some kind of risk when it came to any of Roy's ideas, but he'd become a real asset at the school and in less than a month. "All right. We'll give it a try."

The following morning they revisited the big beachy roost that had launched Lawton and Roy's career in crime. Audrey said to the boys, "No one is going inside that mansion without me.

Understand? I'm not taking any chances of a relapse. Roy, you're staying right here in the truck. Next house it'll be your turn to come with me." Audrey closed the door on him.

He peeped his head out. "Yes, ma'am, but—"

"But *nothing*."

Audrey and Lawton approached the big house and rang the doorbell. A woman opened the door. She didn't recognize Lawton and he barely recognized her. Besides aging, something good had been peeled away. Even the mansion looked exhausted from being the biggest one on the road for so long. Lawton gazed into the house. Overdone wallpaper spun uncontrollably throughout. Sixty-thousand-dollar rugs of midcentury green-and-blue radiation covered the floors. A deluge of pillows were spread across an opulent red velvet sofa offset by expensive vague art by vaguer artists above two silly gilt Empire tables opposite a mandatory Warhol and a cuckoo clock with the wrong time. The ceiling-to-floor window drapes, no longer of first-impression awe, hung with the static motion of someone dead, but it was the air—uncirculated and heavy from too much coughing—that took the life out of the house. Something vile had been inbred and from a lack of restraint it had engulfed everything and left a silence as loud as the void after a truck backfires. The woman, tired and bored, someone who rarely left the upstairs, said, "My children are gone," and shut the door.

Roy stuck his head out the window. "What happened?"

Lawton, getting in the truck, "Twenty years is what happened."

Audrey said to Roy, "I've had enough of your crazy ideas. We're going back to the pool."

An hour later Audrey pulled a sheet of paper from the printer in her small office that was crammed between a water dispenser and a storage room. She walked down the length of the pool and said to Roy, "You remember Wanda? That artist from New York? Got up one morning and took off to LA? Never heard from her again?"

"What about her?"

Showing Roy the printed e-mail. "Found us and our swimming school online."

"We in some kinda trouble?"

"You tell me."

Roy read halfway through when the expression on his face went from concerned to a flash of joy. "She wants to make my movie."

Audrey said, "Read the rest before you celebrate."

He read on. "*Beau?*"

Audrey said, "Your granddad. *Remember* him?"

Roy, wide-eyed and confounded. "She wants to make a film about *old Beau?*"

"Says she already has the script written. Movie takes place on a train. Just needs you to sign the deal to get it green-lighted, whatever that is."

Still confused. "*Old Beau?* How the hell could she get a script written about my granddaddy on a train in a month when she didn't even know old Beau? He been dead longer than she been alive."

"Seems she got enough from your memoir to get it going. Enough to send Lawton a plane ticket to Hollywood."

"She gonna put *Lawton* in the movie?"

"Read the last paragraph."

He did and crunched up the e-mail.

Audrey said, "Isn't that what y'all wanted? Get rich in the movies?"

"I'm the one should be put in the movie. It's my goddamn story. Rangers needed a sharpshooter, they called on Sergeant LaHood, not Lawton Gibbs."

"Well, I don't think it's about how well you handle a weapon, Roy."

"Then you never seen *For a Few Dollars More* with Lee Van Cleef. Changed the whole meaning of what a Western is."

Audrey said, "I didn't know Westerns had any meaning."

"They didn't until the Italians took over what they call the genre. Then the West became a world stuck in time where 'life has no value, but death sometimes has its price.' Not this sentimental machismo bullshit comes outta Hollywood where every movie poster got some pipsqueak with his balls shaved holding a semiautomatic two-fisted SWAT style."

Audrey said, "Well, you can tell Wanda Morris the Cat all about that when you see her. Where's Lawton?"

Roy almost laughed. "I see he told you about her."

"Seems she invited him to a place called the Springs for the weekend. Lawton still hasn't yet made up his mind what to wear. Where is he?"

"Handing out clean towels."

"Show him the e-mail. I don't want him to miss his opportunity of being a whole sensation."

Roy waved for Lawton to come on over. Lawton gave away the last towel and headed to the end of the pool. He could tell by the look on someone's face that he was in big trouble. Roy handed him the e-mail. Lawton read the creased printout. "Have a nice trip, Roy."

"The hell ya mean 'have a nice trip'?"

Audrey said, "Wanda wants to make you a movie star."

"Gonna be girls, money, good times," Roy added, "everything we ever dreamed of."

Audrey said to Lawton, "You could make several hundred thousand dollars."

Roy laughed. "You mean *millions* of dollars. Six figures is chump change over there."

Lawton said, "Maybe it is."

"Maybe *what* is?"

"I'm staying here."

"The hell ya mean you're staying here?"

"What we got is good, Roy. The swimming school is doing fine. Julia is off to college. Crystal is in New York. Crazy Gertie is the hell outta here. And Ronnie Harrison is in big trouble. Things seem to be going right for once."

Roy said with a hint of jealousy, "What's this about Wanda inviting you to her farmhouse?"

Lawton said, "I reckon I'm a little busy at the moment for that."

"Well, she invited me, *too*. So if *you're* going, *I'm* going." Roy snared the e-mail from Lawton and tossed it into the pool.

Audrey said, "You better answer her, Roy. She'll pay you good money for the rights to your memoir, even if the movie's not about you."

"You're damn right she gonna pay. After what Julia took from me, Wanda Morris the Cat gonna pay me double."

Lawton said, "I gave you half my cut in compensation, so I don't know as to why you're complaining. You're not a penny short of nothing."

"No, but *you* are," meaning Hollywood. Roy ambled down the length of the pool mumbling like his teeth were on fire.

He took the older kids to the deep end of the pool. Lawton and Audrey took the younger ones to the shallow side. A seven-year-old girl stared into the water with a determined look on her face. "I wanna swim faster than Michael Phelps."

Lawton said, "You're in the right place, child." Then he heard a ringtone on his phone and swiped his finger across the screen. The text message read: *I'll take u up on that glass of wine.* Lawton looked down the pool where Audrey stood under the halo of midmorning light that poured through the cluster of palm trees that towered over the edge of the pool and beach. A light breeze tipped the pungent Florida air his way. Lawton texted her back with the time and place then put the school whistle to his lips and blew it for the kids, his new life, and the end of ten miserable years.

www.RaederLomax.com

Publishing date: 2016

MIDNIGHT SLEEPER: a prequel to Stand Your Ground, which takes place aboard various Pullman trains.   Sample first page:

CLARKSDALE, MISSISSIPPI   DECEMBER 28, 1925
1
   Morning light poured into the bare cotton fields as Clementine LaHood walked through the back door of her three plow dog trot farmhouse. Freshly picked collards and orange pippins were bunched in her apron. She set them aside on the kitchen table as the first of her children came running down the stairway her husband Beau had promised to fix, the bannister squeaking with each touch of his hand as the children tumbled through the hall and stopped at the kitchen door. An out of breath Western Union boy stood between them and their mother, the telegram already out of his brown leather bag.
   "I'll take that," Beau said as he signed the receipt book and walked around his children who were eyeing the white boy's Western Union Special bicycle by the doorway. Beau handed him a nickel, but his eyes were on the stove top skillet. Clementine put a biscuit in the his hand and shooed him away. Then she turned to Beau, her anger bare. "You can tell the Pullman Company to go to hell."

Made in the USA
Middletown, DE
14 December 2016